Beyond
The
Veil

Kate Allenton

Discover other titles by Kate Allenton

At

www.kateallenton.com

DEDICATION

This book is dedicated to Ilse Shaffer.
I'm thankful for your friendship, more
than you'll ever know.

ACKNOWLEDGMENTS

I'd like to acknowledge my
READERS....You all rock.
Thank you for taking a chance on my
books.

1 CHAPTER

Sophie settled into her new office at Dixon Security, trying to make the space feel a bit more like home by placing a plastic plant in the corner of the almost empty room. She pulled a picture of her and her brother from her purse and set it on her desk. True to Marshall's promise, upon arriving she'd been given keys to a company car; and Ben, the resident IT guy, had taken her on a quick tour of the four- story building where she'd be working. The entire structure, owned by Dixon Security, along with the accompanying parking garage, sat nestled on the other side of town from where she lived. Her new title included Lead Investigator and top dog over Dixon's Psychic Division, and she had the business cards to prove it. It didn't matter that her division contained only one employee or that the other staff members were whispering behind her back. This was her new life, her new reality, and she'd make the most of it.

Ben poked his head into Sophie's office. "I forgot to tell you, Marshall wants to meet with you before the 10 o'clock staff meeting. His office is the last one at the end of the hall. Do you want me to show you?"

"No thanks. I'll find it." A quick glance at her watch told her she'd need to hurry. She had ten minutes until her first official team leader meeting. Her heels were muffled against the carpet as she quickened her pace toward Marshall's office. Thinking she spotted Marshall standing inside the break room, she paused outside and glanced in. A group of men stood inside, yet none of them her boss.

"Damn, you're fine," one of men cooed.

"Sexy as hell," replied another with a wink.

She ignored their comments and the whistles that followed her down the long hall. She kept walking.

Sophie slowed to catch her breath and raised her hand to her stomach to calm the butterflies she'd had all morning. Could she really be doing this? Accountant turned psychic detective had seemed implausible only months ago, but now, it was her reality.

She sidestepped some of the other employees carrying files, and they turned the corner out of sight. The hallway remained quiet and empty by the time she found Marshall's office. Familiar voices spilled out through the open door, penetrating her one-track mind and slowing her step as she neared.

"Fire her," she heard her boyfriend, Jack Love, demand of his best friend. She could just picture him with mused hair, a red face, and the depth of his dark blue eyes.

Surely, he couldn't have been talking about Sophie; surely, he wouldn't dare. She felt the blood rushing up to her cheeks as she took a deep, calming breath.

"Why would I do that?" Marshall protested in a calm, steady voice. "I just hired her."

"You and I both know she isn't cut out for this kind of life."

"She handled herself against Kingston, and that wasn't even with the proper training. Imagine what she can do when she's taught."

Fire filled her veins the longer she listened to Jack's lack of faith in her ability. She'd gone up against a serial killer and won. She'd been the one to prove Kingston was responsible all along. She'd done a more thorough investigation in one month than any of the other cops Jack worked with. How dare he!

"Damn it, Marsh, I'm not playing." Jack's tone hitched in aggravation.

Sophie was about to walk in and demand an apology when she stopped short. His next words left her unable to move, freezing her on the spot.

"I'll give you my sword. Just fire her."

The sting of his offer penetrated her heart. Stomach tightening into knots and not wanting to hear anymore, Sophie stepped out of the shadows and into the doorway. She crossed her arms over her chest as she leaned against the doorframe. Fury heated her cheeks as she balled her fists. He had nerve, balls the size of Texas, and a heart frozen into ice for offering up his prized possession as payment for his demand.

"Jack." Marshall slowly rose from his seat, his eyes wide. He nodded toward the doorway.

Jack glanced over his shoulder, meeting her gaze. There wasn't a tinge of apology in the blue eyes staring back at her, not a word of regret from Jack's mouth. His gaze raked down her body and back up to her face. His jaw set in a clench.

Sophie steeled her resolve and stepped into the room, trying hard to hide the betrayal from her face. Her heart raced as her mind tried to digest how he'd just tried to screw her. She held Marshall's gaze, fighting back the string of forming tears. She pushed her broken emotions to the back of her mind to deal with after work. "We have a meeting in ten minutes."

Marshall nodded and opened his mouth to speak, but Jack stopped him, holding up the palm of his hand. He rose and took a step in Sophie's direction. "Sophie..."

"Don't you Sophie me, you...you...you..." Tongue-tied, she couldn't think of an appropriate name to call the asshole. "How dare you come into

4

my place of employment...*my job*...and suggest that I be fired. What gives you the damn right!"

Sophie took a deep, calming breath, not waiting for his response. She bit the inside of her lip to stave off the tears that began to mist in her vision. She wouldn't give Jack the satisfaction of seeing her cry. Not now and not ever again. Sophie turned to Marshall. "Well? Are you going to take his offer? Should I clean out my office?"

They both turned toward Marshall, waiting expectantly for the decision that would decide her future. She held her breath. Either he wanted the sword, or he wanted her to stay.

Marshall held her gaze as he answered. "I'm afraid I can't do it, Jack." Marshall broke the connection with her and turned to face Jack. "She's under contract."

"Damn it, Marshall, break the fucking contract. We both know you only hired her to get her into bed."

Jack's words cut like a knife through her heart. She couldn't take this. She deserved better from the man she loved. Her crushed heart crumbled, her trust shattered, and all over a damn job he assumed her incapable of handling.

Sophie gave Marshall a curt nod. "I'll be in the conference room with the others."

Straightening her shoulders, she spun on her heels, walked out, and stomped down the hall, leaving Marshall to deal with the asshole.

Sophie stepped into the conference room and paused. Four of the most gorgeous men dressed in fatigues sat around the table. Their eyes pierced her, rooting her in place.

"Seriously?" Had she said that out loud? Her hand flew to cover her mouth as the words slipped free. Heat coursed through her chest and up into her cheeks.

"Come on in, doll." The one closest to her stood and pulled out a chair. "You can sit by me."

Sophie lifted her thumb over her shoulder. "I must be in the wrong room."

More laughter surrounded her as Marshall walked in and ushered her to a seat. "You're in the right room." He waited for the laughter to die down. "Guys, this is Sophie. Sophie, these are my team leaders."

"Marsh, she can work with me." The guy who had pulled out her chair winked at her and held out his hand. "I'm Beau, but you can call me anything you want, darlin'."

She lifted her hand to shake his, but Beau turned it and placed a kiss on the outside of her palm. His lips lingered against her skin.

"Don't let him fool you, sweetheart. He's not that nice, and I'm better endowed," another guy announced.

Beau flew out of his seat, making the guy across the table rise. Beau gave the man a menacing stare, but the other guy's eyes twinkled with mischief, and he lifted his brows in quick succession.

Perfect, another testosterone pissing match. Could her day get any worse?

"Beau, Aiden, sit!" Marshall demanded.

A laugh broke free from Sophie's lips. Maybe from nerves, maybe because of the male perfection sitting around her, maybe because they needed their asses kicked like Jack. Her head throbbed and her body tensed. The heat igniting her veins wasn't lust-induced but from their asinine assumptions that she'd fall for their crap.

"Sophie, I apologize; you would think they've never been around a woman before."

"It's okay, Marshall." She turned to the guys. "Once they get to know me, they'll avoid me like the plague." She turned to Beau and then to Aiden and winked. "I have that effect on men. Just give it time."

"Oh, come on now, honey, that can't be true," the man sitting next to Aiden announced as he leaned back in his chair. "Marshall here wouldn't have hired you if that were the case."

"Are you guys done?" Marshall pegged them each with a glare. "Because we have work to do."

"Sophie, you've met Beau and Aiden..." He gestured to the man sitting next to Aiden. "That's Dash, and the guy sitting at the end is Roman."

Sophie resisted the urge to roll her eyes, unsure if the two quiet ones were going to be just as annoying. Instead she gave a curt nod to them both. Marshall tossed files around the table to all of the men without giving her one. "Here are your new assignments. Review the files and let me know if there are any issues."

Marshall rose. "You four will be working together on this one."

"What about you, boss?" Roman asked.

"Sophie and I will be working a case together. I'll let you know if we need your assistance."

"Aw…." Aiden sighed. "You get all the perks." He wiggled his brow, his gaze riveted to the swells of her breasts.

Marshall tilted his head. "Unless you look good in a cocktail dress, I'm afraid you won't cut it for this assignment, Aiden. This informant only likes women."

Aiden grinned. "I wouldn't mind seeing her in a cocktail dress or better yet seeing it laying on my bedroom floor."

Sophie's head whipped in Aiden's direction. "Really? You want to go there?" She planted her hands on the table and rose. "Let's clear the air, shall we?" She glanced at Marshall, who grinned and nodded to proceed. Standing straighter, she clasped her hands in front of her. "We've established I'm a woman. Get over it. I'm not your mother; I'm not your sister; I won't be fetching your coffee; I'm not sleeping with you; and I don't care who's better endowed. I talk to dead people. I may not be able to beat you in a fight, but I could have them haunt your asses until you're old and gray. I'm here to do a job and I'd like to keep it that way."

Sophie sat back down and let out a long breath.

"Damn, that's hot," Aiden said around his grin. "The kitty has claws."

Sophie rolled her eyes and ignored the arrogant prick.

"Bad day, hun?" Roman asked.

She turned toward the end of the table. "My brother threatened to disown me if I took the job, and my boyfriend just tried to get me fired...so yeah, I guess you could say I've been having a bad day."

Sophie pressed her lips together and shifted her gaze to Marshall. "What's the job?"

"Intel for now."

"She's going to need backup," Roman countered. "When's the meeting?"

"Nine o'clock tonight at Winston's."

"But, boss..."

"I know," Marshall said, cutting him off.

They all nodded as grins split their lips.

"What am I missing?" Sophie asked noticing their grins.

Their grins grew even bigger but none of the jerks answered.

Marshall lifted his brow. "Sophie, I need to see you in my office."

He didn't wait for her reply, just departed from the room with the same air of authority he'd entered. Everyone rose to collect their files acknowledging their dismissal.

"Don't worry, doll, if you need help with the boyfriend or the brother, all you have to do is ask. You're one of ours now, and we protect our own," Aiden announced before leaving the room.

Sophie followed the guys out of the conference room toward Marshall's office. Jack might have wasted his breath trying to get her fired. Her little tirade might have done the trick.

Marshall stood waiting at the door for her and closed it behind them. He gestured to one of the empty chairs before he rounded his desk to sit. "You know Jack didn't mean what he said."

"Jack? That's what you wanted to talk to me about?" she asked incredulously, her cheeks warmed, not from embarrassment but from pure anger at the sound of his name.

He nodded.

"Not my little speech?"

Marshall grinned. "No, they deserved it, and you handled yourself just fine. I want to clear the air about what you overheard."

Sophie pursed her lips and held in the string of expletives she had for her ex-boyfriend, and she did mean *ex*. The prick. "Fine." She perched on the edge of her seat, not even attempting to get comfortable. "He doesn't believe I can do this job. I think he proved that today."

Marshall leaned back in his chair and steepled his fingers in front of him. "Do you know how long I've been after his sword?"

She gave a forced smile and shook her head.

"Ten years, and for ten years he's always told me no, until now...until you. I don't want there to be any confusion between us."

Sophie leaned back in the chair and crossed her legs. "Us?"

Marshall grinned. "Yes, us. I only want us to be honest with each other. I think I've made it clear that I'm attracted to you, but I won't step over the line. Jack offered his sword because he loves you. "

Rising to her feet, she clasped her hands in front of her. "You want honesty?" She'd give him honesty, no holds barred. "Well, let me give you a good dose. Jack offered his sword because he doesn't believe in me. Jack offered his sword because he doesn't want me near you. Jack went behind my back and offered his damn sword because he's selfish. Instead of supporting me, he tried to tear me down, so if you don't mind, I'd rather not talk about Jack. I'd rather talk about our job. What time should I meet you?"

Marshall held her gaze, his green eyes calculating. "Our target is due to show up at the club at around nine. I'll be at your house to pick you up at eight."

She nodded. She could tell there were things he held back from saying just by the dip of his brows. He had more he wanted to explain. Only she held no desire to listen. She'd had enough for the day. Marshall wouldn't understand any more than Jack when he received the earful coming to him. He betrayed her with his actions, and he'd broken her trust. How as she supposed to ignore that?

"I'll be ready."

"Your job tonight is to get the target's attention. I'll do the rest."

2 CHAPTER

Sophie tossed her phone and keys onto the table in the foyer before kicking off her shoes. Unhooking her bra, she padded into her bedroom and sling shot it into the clothes hamper. She had a long night to look forward to, a long night trying to grab some random guy's attention. Her soft blonde hair, blue eyes and modest-sized breasts might do the trick. She sauntered into the bathroom and poked at the heavy bags beneath her eyes. She could do this. It's not as if he'd asked her to sleep with anyone. With enough makeup she could make herself look hot. She smoothed the wrinkles on her face with her hands, the same wrinkles she'd acquired over the last six months. Stunning was not an adjective she'd ever used for herself, yet she'd settle for pretty for the night.

She hurried through her shower, climbed out, and slid into her robe. She twisted her hair up into a towel before plodding into the tiny kitchen in search of food. Jack's assigned ringtone broke through the silence, making her pause. Her stomach recoiled and the ache returned. She stood rooted in place, listening until the last tone died. The sound of a ding filled the room indicating she had a new message. A message she wasn't ready to deal with. Her appetite instantly diminished, so she settled on a bowl of soup, something she could stomach in hopes of getting through the night.

Sophie was slurping at the chicken and noodles when she noticed the familiar glowing ball bouncing from one wall to the next as if in a pinball machine. "Just peachy."

The lights in her kitchen flickered as Will, her spirit guide, drew in the energy from the room and started to form. Her spirit guide. Those words still amazed her. She hadn't even known what that meant six months ago, not to mention that she had one. He'd been a permanent fixture ever since. Normally his visits consisted of a quick morning hello in her head until she mediated, when he'd impart more helpful information. He was her friend, her confidant, and the man she'd personally picked to guide her on her life's quest. And to think, he hadn't warned her against her newly broken heart.

He materialized standing over her and looked down into her bowl. "I'll never understand you. You're here to experience life, and yet you chose to eat that?"

"Some friend you are. You could have warned me," she accused.

"You've tasted it before. Why would I need to warn you?" Will grinned.

"Not about the food, smartass. You could have warned me that Jack's an asshole."

Will's smile slipped. "Sophie...there are things I can't tell you. If you knew everything, there would be no lessons to be learned and no reason for you to stay. Besides, you're the one who wanted him in your chart. You did this to yourself."

"I'm not buying it." Her chart. The bane of her existence, actually the only reason for her existence. She had a hard time imagining that she'd chosen to reincarnate, a mission she'd set for herself, filled with purpose and lessons to be learned. "I must have been on crack. That's the only explanation I can think of if *I* actually wrote him in."

"I assure you that you were not." Will stepped over to her fridge and poked his ghostly head inside without even opening the door.

"Stop that...it's creepy." Sophie shivered.

Will's chuckle filled the small kitchen as he pulled his head back out. "Fine. I came to warn you."

"Oh?" Sophie lowered her spoon back to the bowl. "So you can give me warnings, you just chose not to?"

"Let it go, little bird." Will nodded, his form starting to fade. "Be vigilant, my little friend. Things are often not as they appear."

"Care to elaborate?" she asked, already knowing the answer.

His smirk grew as his body faded out of sight.

"I didn't think so," Sophie whispered into the empty room as she walked over to the sink, dumping her dinner into the garbage disposal and flipping the switch.

Sophie dried her hair, applied her makeup, and slid into the body-hugging undergarments guaranteed to suck in and smooth her extra pounds. The little black dress she squeezed into would have to fit the bill. The material made her feel frumpy, yet it was the best she owned. She slipped on her shoes as the doorbell chimed. Most of her friends just walked in, meaning that whoever stood on the other side of the door didn't feel comfortable enough or know the ritual.

Pulling the door open, she let out a small sigh of relief that Jack wasn't the one waiting. Marshall stood on her stoop dressed in all black. His gaze slid down her body and back up to meet her eyes. "You look beautiful, but I'm afraid that dress isn't going to do."

"Well, you're out of luck, buddy. It's the best I've got."

Marshall handed her a box from behind his back. "I need you to play the part of a spoiled celebrity tonight. The dress and jewelry in the box are part of your cover, and you can keep them when we're done."

"Yum, I didn't know clothes and jewelry were part of the perks." Sophie wiggled her brows, and her lips slid into a grin before she disappeared into her bedroom. She removed the lid and lifted the satin ruby dress out by the spaghetti straps. The length fell to the floor with a slit that would show most of her leg. The dress wasn't like any in her closet. It was sexy and silky and everything she would have never picked out for herself.

"It's beautiful," she hollered through her closed bedroom door as she began to change. She studied her image in the full-length mirror on the back of her door. She felt elegant and classy. She noticed the blue box and her breath caught. Her heart hammered against her chest as she ran her fingers over the embossed lid before opening it. Diamonds sparkled on a necklace nestled on a bed of satin. Matching earrings twinkled next to it. She gently lifted the necklace out, the weight something she hadn't been expecting. She fastened it around her neck and slid the earrings in place.

"We're going to be late," Marshall called out as she opened the door and stepped into the living room.

"I'm ready."

Marshall spun around to face her. His hungry gaze caressed her body, starting at her shoes and working the way up. Every inch of her felt exposed as he took his time until he reached her face. "If you weren't dating Jack, we wouldn't be leaving."

Sophie's cheeks heated and butterflies flipped in her belly. "Are you always this blunt?"

"Yes."

"Good to know." Sophie swallowed her nervousness. "It's the dress."

He closed the distance between them and cupped her cheek with his palm. "No, Sophie...it's not the dress. It's you."

"Marshall."

He cleared his throat, dropped his hand, and stepped back. "I have one more present. Well, it's not really a present, more like something for work."

He pulled out a black sheath holster with a velcro strap. A pearl-handled knife sat nestled inside.

"Where am I supposed to wear that?"

Marshall's lips split into a smile. "On your thigh, of course."

Sophie shrugged and took the knife and holster out of his hands. Placing her foot on her coffee table, she shifted the dress material out of the way.

"Sweet mother of god, you're wearing a garter."

Sophie chuckled as she strapped the holster to her upper thigh. "I like the way they make me feel."

"Damn it, Sophie. You're making this difficult for me to keep my word."

Sophie lowered her leg, letting the dress fall back into place. "I'm sure you'll manage."

"That's easy for you to say."

Sophie grabbed her clutch and keys and walked out the door, leaving Marshall to follow. She felt the heat of his gaze on her backside, so she had no need to turn around to find him checking her out. She tried hard not to fidget as she approached the black stretch limo.

"A limo? Is this necessary?"

He placed his palm on her lower back and steered her toward where Dash stood waiting, dressed up as the limo driver. He had the door open.

"Sophie, you look stunning," Dash complimented, his gaze caressing her body.

"Thanks. I guess you're our backup for the night?"

"The whole team will be there." Marshall announced while sliding next to her on the black leather seat. His arm rested on the seat behind her head. She felt his warmth without his touch. This was her first official job. The excitement produced goose bumps on her arms while she sat nervously waiting like a kid at his first day of school. There wouldn't be any crying tonight.

Jack's ringtone blared from her phone stashed in her clutch. The ringing broke the silence, making her smile slip. She pulled out the phone and answered.

"Hi, Jack." The butterflies in her stomach took flight. She didn't know what to say to him.

"We need to talk."

Her heart fluttered at the smooth silkiness of his voice, her body easily betraying her mind. "I can't right now. I'm working."

"Is he with you?" Jack asked accusingly.

"Yes. We're going to talk to an informant."

A brief silence filled the line before he spoke. "I'll stop by your house later tonight."

"Are you coming by to apologize?"

"I'm not going to apologize for wanting to keep you safe."

Her head fell forward, and she closed her eyes. She should have known it wouldn't be easy with him. Nothing ever was. Something she loved and hated about him. "I can't do this right now."

Marshall's fingers stroked her arm. The move held a silent show of support, nothing remotely romantic.

"Fine." He sighed in frustration. "Just be careful."

Sophie heard the concern lacing his voice. His lack of trust in her abilities squeezed at her heart. "I'll call you later."

An awkward silence followed after she hung up. Marshall remained unusually quiet.

"Sorry about that," she replied as the limo pulled into a parking lot and stopped in front of the small club she'd never been inside before. The neon sign above the entrance flashed a woman leaning against a pole. "Is this a strip club?"

Marshall gave her a hesitant glance. "Not exactly, but if you have to ask, I take it you've never been here before?"

Her gaze returned to the window as she shook her head. She didn't have a clue what she was walking into.

"Well then, you're in for a treat."

Dash opened Sophie's door and held out his hand, and she clasped his fingers as she stepped out. Her eyes scanned the parking lot, taking in the scene around them. Several women in groups walked by with their arms entwined as they headed toward the bouncer at the door. Laughter and people surrounded them. The sound of two women arguing came from nearby. Marshall placed his hand on her lower back and escorted her to the door.

Leaning into her ear, he whispered. "You aren't my arm candy tonight, sugar. Just consider us your security and the target will seek you out."

Sophie nodded. "What does he look like?"

"The description given to me included hair as black as midnight, eyes the color of sapphires, and a voice that can reach your soul," he whispered as he nodded to the bouncer, who let them pass. "Don't worry." He winked. "I'm confident she'll find you."

"She!" Sophie's mouth dropped open.

Marshall's grin turned big. "It's a gay bar, mostly women"—he shrugged—"and some swingers."

Sophie pursed her lips. "Well, you're going to stick out like a sore thumb."

Marshall chuckled. "The whole team will. If anyone asks, we're your muscle."

They walked through the door into the darkened room. Elaborate booths lined the walls along with tables near the stage. A spotlight was pointed toward the woman standing on the stage crooning out a slow song as crowds gathered around. Beau lingered near the bar while the rest of the team leaders surrounded an empty table in the VIP section.

He leaned in. "I'll get us some drinks. Why don't you head to the table, and don't be afraid to let out your inner kitten."

Kitten? She wasn't told she had to provide a kitten. How was she supposed to do kitten when she was uncomfortable and hyper aware of the gazes that raked her as she passed? She took a deep, calming breath hoping to dig deep to find the confidence she'd need tonight. She sashayed, with an extra swing in her hips, as she made her way through the club. She batted her lashes and displayed a small smile on her lips. She spotted the target immediately and held the woman's gaze as she rounded the bar. The woman was sitting on a man's lap, and she moved her hips against his crotch while a blonde woman kissed her neck. The man ran his hands over the woman's breasts, rubbing his fingers against her nipples. The dark-haired woman threw her head back, and her chest heaved as she hurried her movement against the man's lap.

Alrighty then. Sophie could do this. It was just a job. Moistening her lips, Sophie held the brunette's gaze as she passed, winking in an attempt to look sexy and not as nerdy as she felt.

Aiden greeted her, his palm on her arm as he leaned in to kiss her cheek. "I think she took the bait. But next time don't act so easy."

"Easy? I don't know how to flirt with women."

He winked as he helped her into the booth. "Don't worry. I do and I'll give you tips."

"Just what I need, flirting tips from Don Juan." What the hell had she gotten herself into?

Marshall returned moments later with drinks. He set a glass topped with fruit and an umbrella down in front of her, while he held onto his beer. He slid into the booth beside her as his gaze scanned the crowd. He leaned in to whisper into her ear.

"You need to get her to the limo."

"And then what?" Sophie asked, trying to hide the trepidation in her voice.

"We'll take it from there."

Sophie turned her gaze to the dance floor when a DJ started to play a popular song. Two women were in the middle; their bodies pressed together, their hips gyrating to the hypnotic song.

Their hands caressed up and down each other's bodies the way lovers might. They swayed while their mouths embraced in a passionate kiss.

Aiden stood rigid behind her booth. He leaned down next to her ear and whispered, "Kind of hot isn't it?"

"If you're into that," she answered through her fake smile. Every hair on her arm stood on end as Marshall slid closer to her. His body pressed against her side.

"We have an audience," he whispered the moment his palm caressed her thigh.

Her thighs quivered at his touch. This was wrong; this was all wrong. She was in a gay bar and she had a boyfriend.

"I thought you said you were security." She turned to Marshall, and the fine lines of his face tightened. She saw the rising lust building in his eyes.

Marshall leaned into her, his breath hot against her neck. "Our target is a swinger. We need to up the ante."

He rested his palm against her cheek, and his eyes softened with a look of apology.

His palm stilled her from turning to look, his breath a whisper against her lips. "Don't look." He caressed her cheek, trailing his fingers down her neck. He cupped her neck. "I'm going to kiss you now, and it would help if you acted like you're enjoying it."

"Is this for her or for you?" Sophie asked as goose bumps gathered on her skin.

His hungry gaze dropped to her lips. Uncertainty clouded his face.

"As much as I've wanted to do this, Soph, this kiss is work." His heated gaze pierced her soul, contradicting his words. "Until you tell me otherwise."

Turmoil waged in her mind as he pressed his warm lips to hers. She stiffened beneath his touch before she remembered to play her part. She relaxed and let him take the lead. His tongue stroked hers lips and she opened in invitation. He delved inside, sipping and tasting as he brushed his tongue against hers, deepening the kiss. He took his time, as if savoring her taste, while he explored her mouth. She moaned, ashamed of what it meant. Heat flared inside her, making her ache while her mind struggled to remember this was an operation and Marshall was her boss.

He broke the kiss, his forehead leaning against hers, his breath coming in slow pants. "I shouldn't have done that." He closed his eyes. "I should have figured out a different way."

The music stopped, and the room became silent as the lights dimmed further. Sophie tried to stifle the butterflies in her belly as she turned to the stage. Her target stood beneath the spotlight. Her black shiny hair hung down to her waist. She riveted her gaze on Sophie and Marshall as the woman licked her lips. She opened her mouth and began to sing.

A soulful blues song echoed in the air, each melody and note full of emotion and aimed at Sophie as she held her gaze. The words in the song accused of betrayal and lust, the implication stabbing like a knife into Sophie's chest. She'd just cheated on Jack. Although the kiss had been meaningless, she hadn't pushed Marshall away. Jack didn't deserve that. Did that make him right? Was she unable to handle the job?

"I can't do this," Sophie announced as she struggled with her inner turmoil.

"Sophie, wait." Marshall grabbed for her, but she twisted free, hurrying out of the booth. She headed for the bathrooms, a place to be alone to regain the control that she severely lacked tonight.

She pushed open the door and took a deep breath. The scent of roses drifted to her nose. Vases full of flowers sat on the sink. The expansive bathroom was decorated in expensive tile with a soft floral pattern print on the walls. The decorations opposed the feel of the bar, as if transporting her into another place.

Sophie stepped up to a sink and gripped the porcelain tight with both hands. She stared at herself in the mirror. Her mind raced with the implications of her job and the kiss. She needed to tell Jack.

The door opened up behind her, and the black-haired singer held her gaze in the mirror's reflection as she walked into the room. "You know, Sophie....I would have pegged you more for Jack's type than Marshall's."

The singer knew him? More than that, she knew all of them? Sophie spun around. "Do I know you?"

The woman grinned as she sashayed to the counter, two sinks down. She spread lipstick on her lips and pressed them together before she answered. "No, but I know you."

The woman turned and leaned her hip against the counter. "He said you would come and"—she grinned—"here you are."

Sophie shook the confusion from her mind. "Who said I would come?"

She tsked. "Afraid I can't tell you that, honey, but that scorching kiss told me enough. Your man sure knows how to kiss."

She fanned her chest and lifted a finger to her lips. "I can still taste him." She winked. "It's a pity really..."

"What is?"

"That you got pulled into this game. You don't even know who's pulling the strings. Do you?"

"Why don't you tell me?" Sophie's blood boiled at the thought of anyone screwing with her life. She fisted her hands at her sides, ready to kill.

She stepped closer to Sophie, invading her space. She trailed her red-painted fingernail down Sophie's arm. "Afraid I can't do that, Sophie. I'd like to keep my life."

The woman winked before strolling out.

Sophie's head clouded as she replayed the conversation in her mind. "What the hell just happened here?"

She yanked the door open and stormed out of the bathroom. Her gaze scanned over the crowd searching for the woman she'd just met, intent to get some much needed answers. She was nowhere to be found. Marshall stood next to the table, wiping red lipstick from his mouth.

Sophie felt eyes on her as she made her way to the table. The hair on Sophie's neck prickled in unease. One look into Marshall's eyes told her that he hadn't a clue. "Which way did she go?"

Aiden tilted his head. "She went into the bathroom with you. I haven't seen her come out of the hall."

"We need to find her. We've been played."

Sophie lifted the hem of her dress and hurried back to the hallway, which had several doors. She opened the men's room, the space empty other than the urinals hanging on the walls. That didn't surprise her. She opened the next door to find it full of supplies. Marshall stood behind her as she pushed open the back exit door. A trail of dust and smoke greeted them, choking them as taillights zoomed out of sight.

As she turned to go back inside, she spotted the legs poking out from behind the open door. Someone had propped the woman up against the brick wall. Her eyes were wide open in fear, and she had a bullet wound through the head and a knife shoved in her chest. *This isn't happening. Not again.* Sophie choked down the bile rising in her throat and covered her mouth with her hand.

"Marshall," she called toward his retreating back. "We have a problem."

3 CHAPTER

Sophie pulled Dash's jacket tighter around her body, fighting against the chill of the cool night breeze as the coroner and police worked the scene. Marshall stood off in the distance, Jack on one side of him and Sophie's brother, Max, the police chief, on the other. She didn't have to be part of the conversation to know what words were being exchanged. Her brother pointed a finger in her direction while arguing with Marshall. Jack stood next to them with his arms crossed over his chest and a scowl on his face.

Somehow this was all her fault. Somehow it always was. Sophie lowered her head, a headache forming and piercing behind her eyes. She'd given her statement to one of the other officers, though a lot of good that did. She looked guilty having been the last person to see the singer alive.

"It's not your fault," the ghost of the black-haired woman announced as she appeared beside her. "It's theirs." The ghost glanced over toward where Marshall and Jack stood.

"What does that even mean?" Sophie asked. The fact a ghost stood in front of her would shock others, yet it didn't shock her. The appearances were par for the course in Sophie's life. They appeared out of nowhere and would disappear just as quickly.

Sad eyes stared back at Sophie. The apparition started to fade without answering the question.

Sophie released a deep breath and slowly maneuvered through the crowds to where the others stood. All conversation ceased as she neared. Jack's gaze started at her feet and travelled up her body, the lines of his mouth pulled into a fine line. Right now, she didn't care. Right now, she just wanted to get this over with and go home.

"Can I go home?" she asked her brother, ignoring Jack completely.

"Did you give your statement?" Max questioned.

She nodded as exhaustion filled her body.

"Is there anything else you want to tell us?" Max asked.

Sophie met Jack's unrelenting gaze. She needed to tell him about the kiss. She wanted to confess it all, but not here and not in the presence of her brother or their coworkers. "No."

****

Sophie's shoulders sagged, and her red-rimmed eyes hinted at her physical and mental exhaustion. Jack wanted to pull her into his arms, wanted to wipe the memory of their previous fight out of her mind, but just couldn't do it. She stood in a silky red dress out on a date with Marshall. Every part of him wanted to believe it was just work, yet he knew he was wrong. Marshall had held her wrapped in his arms when he and the other cops had arrived on scene, comforting her over a death that she shouldn't have even witnessed. He wanted to strangle both of them.

"I'll take you home," Marshall announced.

"Like hell you will," Jack growled. "I'm taking her home."

Sophie held up her hands. "Let's not do this." She shook her head. "Marshall, I'll see you at the office tomorrow and Jack"—she glanced over to him—"I still don't need your protection."

Sophie spun on her heels and headed back in the direction of the front parking lot.

"Sophie, wait." Jack jogged up beside her before slowing to match her gait. "How are you going to get home?"

"Aiden."

The words had barely left her lips, and Jack had already flexed his fingers in an attempt to mask his response. Aiden was a womanizer. Jack knew it; why couldn't Sophie see it. "Sophie, I'm sorry."

She rounded the corner of the club to the parking lot. His words made her pause. She crossed her arms over her chest. "Jack…"

He pulled her into his arms and kissed her like a man starved. He put every ounce of passion into it, hoping that it might convince her. When he broke the kiss, she leaned her head against his chest.

"Let me take you home, Sophie. We don't have to talk. I just want to hold you."

"Is this the boyfriend who tried to get your sweet ass fired?" Aiden asked from behind Jack. He would have turned around and decked the asshole had Sophie not had her palm on his arm.

"Can you take me home, Aiden?"

"Sure, honey." Aiden smirked and held out his hand to Sophie. "I'll tuck you into bed and everything."

Sophie patted Jack's chest and stood on her tiptoes to kiss his cheek. "We do need to talk, but not tonight. Okay?"

Jack reluctantly agreed and watched her walk off with another man. Aiden tried to put his arm around her shoulder and she smacked him in the gut. Her actions should have made Jack happy, but he knew deep down in his gut, he'd screwed up. His heart clenched as he watched her leave, knowing nothing would ever be the same between them.

****

The next morning, Sophie stepped into the conference room to find all of the guys waiting for her. The men in the room were all quiet, their watchful gazes never missing a beat. She pulled out a chair and sat down. Picking up her pen, she tapped it on her notebook.

"Good morning." She folded her arms on the table. "Seems we have a bit of a problem."

Aiden chuckled. "It's the boyfriend, isn't it? He's intimidated by me."

"Hardly."

She swung her gaze to the head of the table and leaned back in her chair. "Who hired you for last night's operation?"

Marshall's brows dipped. "That's confidential."

"Confidential or not, we were set up."

"How do you know?" normally quiet Roman asked.

"Dead girl from the bathroom told me." She spun her gaze back to Marshall. "After you kissed her."

He held up his hands. "She kissed me."

Sophie shook her head, trying to fight the forming headache. "That's so not the point."

"I think it is," Aiden replied.

"Was she dead when she told you?" Beau asked.

"She was alive when she left the bathroom. I didn't see her spirit until the police were on the scene."

"What? When?" Marshall asked.

Sophie rubbed at her temples. "When Jack and my brother were yelling at you about getting me involved."

"Wait." Aiden held up his hand. "Your brother is..."

"The police chief," she answered, not waiting for him to put the pieces together.

"That puts a damper on things," Dash whispered from the other side of the room.

She shook her head. "Stay focused, guys. Her ghost appeared and told me that it's not my fault."

"Well, we already knew that," Marshall added.

"She told me Jack and you were to blame. Do you care to enlighten us?" Sophie asked, gesturing to encompass the others in the room.

Marshall placed his elbows on the table, closed his eyes, and pinched the bridge of his nose, his calm facade not quite cracking but dissolving nonetheless.

The conference room door flew open, banging against the wall. "You fucking bastard."

Jack looked ready to explode. His cheeks were bright red, his glare menacing as he clenched his fists. He tossed a picture into the middle of the table and Sophie's breath caught. A blown-up, glossy picture of Marshall kissing her at the club stared back at her.

"I'm sorry. I couldn't stop him," Claire, the receptionist, announced from behind him, her look apologetic.

Marshall rose from his seat as Jack headed in his direction.

"Dude." Beau propelled out of his chair in a flash, stepping between them. "This isn't the place, and you're outnumbered."

Jack's jaw clenched when he turned to her. She could read the disappointment in his eyes, the anger and betrayal, both emotions she'd felt yesterday.

"It's not what you think," she answered before picking up the picture and turning to him. "Where did you get this?"

"What does it matter? Are you mad that your secret's out, princess?" he asked accusingly. "Are you screwing him too?"

Marshall stepped around Beau, confronting Jack face to face. "You're going down a road you'll regret, Jack. She doesn't deserve that shit, and you know it."

He turned his glare to Marshall. "Do I?"

Roman, Dash, and Aiden rose from their chairs, the testosterone thick in the air. Anger welled up in her chest, making it hard to breathe. Jack didn't know her; hell, none of them did. Sophie tossed the picture onto the table and shook her head. "Screw you, Jack."

Her vision started to blur and the room started to spin. She heard them call her name as she whispered, "Not again."

****

She opened her eyes to find a white ceiling above her. A quick glance around confirmed she'd never been there before. When she'd first started fainting, she always ended up in a meadow, surrounded by flowers and deceased spirits; nothing like this place. The white walls lacked any décor and the room appeared sterile. She eased herself up on the white couch; the white chair across from her was the only other furniture in the room.

"Hello," Sophie called out as she rose, hoping for the best but preparing for the worst. It was never a good sign when the spirits pulled her wherever they liked to bring her. She waited and wondered who she'd be visiting this time around.

A guy appeared in the chair across from her. A man she'd never seen before. "Who are you?"

He shrugged. "Everyone and no one."

She clenched her eyes shut. "Really? I'm sure you're all saintly and stuff, but could we not play games?"

"I didn't bring you here."

Her eyes popped open and she shook her head. This ghost seemed confused. She hadn't sought him out.

Will, she called in her head. No one answered.

Sophie crossed her arms over her chest and let her gaze linger on the ghost in front of her. His form turned solid as if he were someone she could reach out and touch. He was good looking, albeit in a surfer kind of way. Definitely not her type, even if he were alive. He ran a hand through his already tousled wavy blond hair. His genuine smile highlighted the creases around his blue eyes. A scar marred the left side of his neck. He had a small tattoo inked on his right wrist.

"Okay, everyone and no one; what was your name when you were alive?"

"Ryan," he answered, his lips tilted in a smile as he gestured to the couch.

"No, I think I'll stand."

He gave a slight nod. "Suit yourself."

"Why am I here?"

Ryan shrugged and settled his ankle on his opposite knee, as if he were getting comfortable. "I don't know. I'm assuming it has something to do with you yelling at my two best friends."

"Come again?" Sophie plopped down onto the couch, more confused than she'd been in a long time.

He dropped his foot to the floor and leaned forward, resting his elbows on his knees. "I guess they've never mentioned me?"

"No." Sophie saw the hurt in the spirit's eyes before he masked it from her view.

"Well, it's been fifteen years so I shouldn't be surprised." He stood. His large frame towered over hers as he glanced around the room. "I shouldn't be here."

She stood. "I'm pretty sure you're right where you belong. I'm the one who shouldn't be here."

He shook his head. "No...I shouldn't be here. I shouldn't be telling you this."

Sophie couldn't hide the confusion on her face. "I think you're pretty safe. You haven't told me crap."

He placed his cold palms on her arms. "They're in danger."

Sophie's brow rose at the thought of the chaos she'd disappeared from. Jack *was* in danger of her right hook. "Yeah, you can say that again."

He shook his head. "You don't understand."

"Story of my life, buddy."

His once-solid form started to fade. "He's coming for them, just like he did me."

Ryan disappeared from her sight and her head started to spin.

She walked back over to the couch and lay down, closing her eyes. "Beam me up, Scotty."

The hair all over her body rose as the tingling feeling started in her fingers, working its way up through her arms, the process of being sucked back into the void to reappear where she'd left. A place where, in all honesty, she didn't care to be.

Her eyes flew open to find Jack and Marshall hovering over her.

"Who the hell is Ryan?" she asked accusingly. "And how in the hell did he die?"

4 CHAPTER

Sophie pushed herself to sit up, brushing away the hands trying to help. Her gaze swept the room making sure the others hadn't followed. She watched Marshall and Jack exchange a worried glance, neither of them answering her questions.

She rose to her feet. Marshall and Jack stared back at her with a lethal calmness. She knew that look. They remained tight lipped. The silence told her all she needed to know. They weren't going to tell her zip.

"Blond hair, blue eyes, oh, I don't know..." Tilting her head, she crossed her arms over her chest. "Claimed to be your best friend."

The sound of a pin dropping could have been heard while she waited. Not the typical reaction she normally got from these two. She gave a firm nod, the walls around her heart slowly building back into place.

"More secrets, just perfect." Sophie took a deep, calming breath and plastered a fake smile on her face. "Well, I have a lunch date I'm late for, so..." She pulled at the hem of her shirt, straightening it as she headed for the door. "When you two figure out who he is, let me know." She pulled the door open, her hand resting on the knob. "Jack..." She held back the tears forming in her eyes. "We only kissed because of my cover. I"—she clenched her eyes closed before opening them to meet his gaze—"hope one day you learn how to trust, even if it's not with me." She tilted her head to Marshall. "You two used to be thick as thieves. I never intended to come between you."

Sophie quietly closed the door, not caring what they discussed. Her determination, for a quick exit out of the building before the waterworks started, sat like a rock in her belly. She eased her phone out of her pocket and shot off a simple text, letting her best friend know she'd be five minutes late leaving. Sophie turned the corner into her office, pausing mid-step. Two pairs of eyes met hers. Aiden sat reclined in her chair with his feet propped up on the desk, his fingers laced and resting on his stomach, wearing a mischievous grin on his face. He gave her a saucy wink. Beau was sitting in another chair, his legs crossed at the ankles and his hands propped behind his head.

"Do we need to kill them?" Aiden asked.

Yes. No. She warred with herself until, ultimately, she shook her head. Remembering what Ryan had said about them being in trouble was the ultimate deciding factor. No matter how mad she'd been at them, they were going to need her help. "No, but I need a favor."

"Want us to rough them up for you? We can take them."

A spark of hope grew in her heart as she grabbed her purse. Her new purpose and determination sprouted wings like a baby bird about to jump from the nest. "How about I buy you guys lunch and we can talk about it."

Aiden and Beau were out of their seats in mere seconds. They were easily enticed.

"Lunch with a fine woman? You know I'm in," Aiden replied.

"You offered two of our favorite things," Beau agreed. "Life doesn't get any better than that unless you eat in the buff."

"Sadly no, but today's your lucky day....two women for the price of one and the best Mexican you'll ever taste." She patted his chest and headed for the door. "And you don't even have to pick up the tab. Let's go."

****

Sophie's large SUV felt cramped with Aiden riding shotgun and Beau in the backseat. They joked with each other the entire way, trying to entice a lighter mood. Her mind was replaying her miserable morning in an unbreakable loop while searching for answers just out of her reach. She parked along the curb at the front entrance of the restaurant, pulling in right behind her best friend's car. The tiny street in the practically deserted part of town was quiet and unassuming, her own little oasis where the mass of tourists and the working crowd remained elusive.

"This place looks abandoned," Aiden announced as he unfolded his legs and climbed out of the SUV.

"Are you sure it's a restaurant?" Beau asked, shutting his door. His gaze roamed the building, not a sign in sight to indicate what business might lie inside.

Aiden glanced up and down the street. If Sophie had to guess, he was making a quick assessment of his situation.

Sophie grinned and rounded the SUV. "Are you scared?" she called over her shoulder and chuckled as she walked into the restaurant that she and her best friend had found only a year ago. Beau and Aiden might be used to exclusive gun ranges and bars, but Sophie and Amber knew where to find the best food and margaritas in town.

The guys followed behind Sophie, who greeted her best friend sitting at the only occupied table in the joint. Her brunette hair was hanging in loose curls around her face and shoulders. Her chocolate eyes held a tint of mystery. The darkened restaurant was quiet save for the light Mexican music playing in the background like elevator music. Sombreros lined the green and yellow walls. The vinyl-covered tables had seen better days, and the covers on the booths could have used some repair. None of the decorations deterred her from eating at the place. The owner was sweet, the food was excellent, and the margaritas were to die for.

Amber's mouth parted and she sat a little straighter and smoothed down her hair. She grinned and bit her bottom lip when she noticed Sophie's company.

Sophie winked.

"You brought me presents?" She gleamed as Sophie slid into the opposite side of the booth. Aiden sat next to Sophie, leaving Beau to sit with Amber.

"Beau, Aiden....meet Amber; she's the female version of you." Sophie chuckled. "Only she can cook and clean."

The guys' gazes went back and forth from Amber to her, humor etched into the fine contours of their faces.

Beau rested his arm on the booth behind Amber's head. "You do realize how awesome we are, don't you?"

Sophie's smile broadened. "She's better. The only difference is she can't kick your ass, but I'm hoping we can fix that."

Raul, the owner and bartender, walked over to the table, setting a margarita down in front of Amber. "Ah, Miss Sophie, I was hoping you'd be joining Amber today. Would you care for your usual margarita?"

"Not today, I'm afraid. I have to go back to work. How about a sweet iced tea?"

Raul nodded. "And for your gentleman friends?"

They each ordered a beer and watched as Raul walked off.

Amber licked the salt off the rim of her glass before taking a sip of her margarita; after her first sip, she purred, mimicking the sound a satisfied kitten makes after being stroked. Aiden and Beau were mesmerized, as though they'd witnessed an Oscar performance.

"I bet I can get her to make that sound again without the help of alcohol," Beau exclaimed.

"Do you purr, Sophie?" Aiden asked as he inched closer to her side.

Sophie ignored them both and smiled at her best friend.

"Okay, what gives? It's not my birthday." She turned to winked at Beau. "But if it were, you two would be the best presents ever. So, to what do I owe the honor?"

Aiden tossed his arm around Sophie's shoulders and gave a light squeeze. "Sophie's had a crap day."

"Whose balls do I need to kick?" She grinned and turned to Beau, running her hands up and down his arm, stroking his muscles like they were his ego. "You'll bail me out of jail, won't you, sugar?" she asked in her seductive voice before blowing him a kiss.

Beau blushed, making Aiden chuckle. "She is good."

"I told you," Sophie agreed before taking control of the conversation. From the look on Amber's face, it was just a matter of time before she had them both eating out of the palm of her hand. "Jack thinks I'm sleeping with Marshall."

Aiden shrugged. "Well, in his defense, he did see a picture of you two in a lip-lock."

Sophie smacked Aiden's abs and her hand came away throbbing. "It was work, nothing more."

"How do I get a job like that?" Amber asked with a grin.

Raul arrived with their drinks. "Do you know what you want to eat?"

Sophie met Amber's gaze. They both grinned and answered together. "Nachos."

Raul walked off to start their order.

Beau was right. The picture looked worse than what had actually happened, but Jack should have trusted her reasons and at least given her the chance to explain, instead of barging in and making a scene. The memory was a painful reminder of the sorrow she'd been feeling lately.

"No frowning." Aiden squeezed her shoulder again. "This is a fun lunch."

"You sound like Amber when we went to Salem. She lied too."

"Don't let her fool you. We had fun." Amber took another sip of her drink and moaned. Both men's eyes spun toward her. "What?" she asked. "It's better than sex."

"Then you don't have the right partner." Beau chuckled. He moved his arm beneath the table and Amber's breath caught. She nailed him with a raised brow in question before a smile split her lips. Tilting her head, Sophie watched as Amber's arm moved too.

Amber cleared her throat. "What else happened?"

Sophie took a sip of her tea, wishing it was something stronger. "Let's see....I was taken to a swingers bar, kissed by my boss, a woman died, her ghost visited me, and then after the big confrontation with Jack during our meeting today, another spirit decided to pull me away for a chat."

"You need this more than me." Amber brought her hands back on top of the table and pushed her margarita over in front of Sophie.

Sophie pushed it back. "Come over around seven and bring a bottle."

"Honey, it's Friday. I'll bring two." Amber winked.

"If you're going to have pillow fights, you can count us in," Aiden announced and fist-bumped Beau.

"Yeah....no. I think I've had my daily allowance of testosterone."

"Okay, then tell me why we're here if it's not to clean your pipes," Aiden said. "Because we'd do a damn fine job. We've been known to fulfill a fantasy or two." Aiden wiggled his brows in quick succession.

Amber fanned her face and rubbed her hand up and down Beau's bicep. "Can't we keep them? I promise I'll be good." She grinned. "Or really, really bad."

"I'm voting really, really bad," Beau answered.

Sophie smiled, comfortable now. She'd needed this distraction. The banter and playfulness of friends eased her restless soul. "No." She glanced at Aiden to find his gaze steady on her. "Okay, here's the deal..."

Food arrived, interrupting her announcement. Raul set four huge plates of nachos in front of them and they all started to dig in.

Sophie picked up a chip and took a bite. The melted cheese dripped down her chin, and before she could reach a napkin, Aiden brushed his finger over it, wiping the mess away. He winked then sucked his finger into his mouth.

Rolling her eyes, Sophie picked up her tea and sipped. "Okay, here's the deal. I already know how to shoot, but I need to learn how to protect myself."

Aiden and Beau shared a look. "Protect yourself from what?"

Sophie shrugged. "From whoever killed that woman last night. She told me it was a setup. Hell, she even knew my name. I have a feeling whatever this is, it's just getting started and if it's aimed at Jack and Marshall then I'm going to be a prime target."

Aiden's lips pulled into a thin line, his tone serious. "When do we start?"

Sophie's heart felt as though it had started beating again. She'd no longer have to trust Marshall or Jack to watch her back if she could do it herself. With Aiden's tutelage, she could handle it on her own.

"Well….I was thinking since there is a gym and sparring area at the office, maybe we could start today after I get off?"

"You need help with that?" Aiden asked.

"With what?"

"Getting off," Aiden replied. A mischievous smile twisted on his lips. His fingers landed on her arm, no longer on the seatback. He lightly brushed his finger up and down her shoulder.

Sophie clenched her eyes shut. Maybe this had been a bad idea from the start. She needed more flirting and men like she needed a hole in her head.

"I'm sorry." Aiden removed his hand and eased into her side, knocking her like a friend would. "I'll keep it strictly PG, unless of course you beg me for it."

"Don't hold your breath, hot shot. Sophie doesn't beg," Amber replied for her.

"You already know how to shoot, and the bone head over there is going to teach you to fight. What do you need me for?" Beau asked.

Sophie cleared her throat, her gaze going between Beau and Amber. "Do you mind teaching Amber to shoot? She is my best friend, and that's a dangerous job."

Amber's eyes bulged and she turned to Beau, excitement radiating from her voice. "I'm a quick learner. Would you really do that?"

"I'll pay both of you," Sophie announced.

Beau shook his head and his gaze turned playful as he stared into Amber's eyes. "No payment necessary. I'd love to teach this little spitfire to kill."

He lowered his head and captured her lips in a kiss that would have melted the hearts of any woman around.

When he pulled back, Amber still had her eyes closed and her lips tilted in a smile. "Yeah...." She turned to Sophie and opened her eyes. "He should be the one to help me."

Sophie couldn't hold in her chuckle. "I hope you teach as fast as you go in for the kill."

****

Sophie returned from lunch to find both Marshall and Jack gone. Their absence lightened the atmosphere, allowing her to go about the rest of the day without worry of one of them barging into her office.

True to Aiden's words, he'd remained a gentleman while putting her through a grueling training session. Her entire body ached when she moved, each step a painful memory of the hell she'd endured. Training might have been the wrong decision. She should have started with some Pilates, maybe yoga to break in her muscles. Even that may have been too much. A walk around the block could have sufficed. Leave it to her to pick an ex-marine to give her a workout. Determination or mental illness, she hadn't figured which, had her agreeing to another round on Saturday morning. Sophie used the shower facilities in the building before packing up and going home. The hot water soothed her aching muscles.

Ben, the computer nerd, walked her out since they left at the same time. He'd told her not to worry about the scene Jack had caused, that in time the other employees would forget. Sophie blushed at the thought. He wished her a great weekend and got into his car and left. She called in her order for her and Amber before she ever pulled out of the lot. If her plan was to drink, and drink heavily, she'd need the food to soak it up.

She'd just walked in her home and changed into her comfy yoga clothes and a tank top, her preferred after-work attire, when a knock sounded on her door.

"Why did you knock?" she asked as she yanked the door open, thinking maybe Amber had lost her mind or her hands were full. The person standing on the other side wasn't her best friend who'd promised to bring the liquor. Instead, it was the accuser himself. Jack Love stood on her porch. "What are you doing here?"

He ran a hand through his short brown hair. Unease written all over his face, he heaved out a heavy sigh. "I think we should have that talk now."

She crossed her arms over her chest, the move lifting her boobs. She didn't do it on purpose, but out of habit. If his hands touched her, they wouldn't be talking at all. He'd have her pinned to the wall and nothing would be accomplished. His gaze zeroed in on the swells of her breasts showcased by the tight tank top. She snapped her fingers. "Eyes up here."

His lips split into a grin. "Sorry."

"No, you're not."

"No, I'm not." His grin grew bigger. "Can I come in?"

Sophie hesitated, not in the mood for another argument. "Are you ready to tell me who Ryan is?"

He shook his head. "No."

She stepped back, allowing him entrance against her better judgment. She closed the door and followed him into the living room. "Jack..."

He turned and shook his head. "Sophie, let me go first."

Nervously, she moistened her dry lips, meeting his gaze. She nodded her consent while swallowing around the boulder lodged in her throat.

"I'm sorry. I was a jackass and I shouldn't have assumed anything. It's just I know Marshall and how persistent he can be." Jack turned his back to her and paced to the other side of the room. "Then I saw the picture and I lost it." He spun back around to face her. "I don't want to lose you. Tell me you didn't feel anything when he kissed you. Tell me that and I'll believe you."

His expression softened as he waited for an answer. An answer she was dreading to give.

"I'm sorry that it happened." Her gaze dropped to her feet. The next words out of her mouth were the hardest she'd ever say. "But I can't tell you that I didn't feel anything. I did, and although it was different than your kiss, I'd be lying if I told you it didn't affect me. I've never lied to you and I won't start now, but you should have let me explain. It was work. I love you and you should have trusted that, trusted me."

Jack's jaw clenched and his body stiffened. She stood motionless in the middle of the room, watching and waiting for the next explosion to hit, the verbal sparring to commence.

"You were right about one thing though." She took a deep breath. "I wasn't prepared for this job, and it's no one's fault but my own. I may have been naïve accepting the job, but I know I can make a difference and help people, and I'm not quitting. Not when I've found my purpose."

"Not even for me?"

She took an abrupt step toward him and then paused.

"If you loved me, you wouldn't ask. You'd support my decision."

Jack closed the distance between them in two long strides, resting his warm palm on her arm. He crooked his finger to lift her chin. His gaze searched hers as if trying to read her soul. "I do love you, and that's why I'm asking."

God how she wanted to believe that, to believe what he was telling her was the truth, but his actions contradicted his words. He'd tried to get her fired, he'd accused her of sleeping with Marshall without even talking to her, and he wouldn't come clean about Ryan. His definition of love was slightly twisted and different from hers, and she couldn't seem to fill the gap. Not without lying to herself and him.

She stepped back and watched his hands fall to his sides. Confusion clouded his face, yet she needed the distance to strengthen her resolve. "I wish that were true."

She wanted nothing else but to walk back into his arms and tell him that everything would be okay, to let him kiss her worries away, but she just couldn't bring herself to do it.

"Damn it, Sophie; it is true, and you kissed him."

"I'm sorry, Jack. I'm sorry about the kiss and that I put myself in the position. I'm sorry I didn't tell you about it that night. There are a hundred and one things I should have done differently, but none of that will fix this. Fix the real problem." The pressure and sadness in her chest was making it hard to breathe. She needed a clear head if what Ryan said was true. Marshall and Jack needed more from her than a warm body in either of their beds. That fact and that fact alone made the words sour as they left her mouth, words she'd never thought to speak. She approached him and placed her hand on his chest. "Jack...I need time to sort this all out and find my place."

A knock sounded on her door before it swung open. Marshall walked in, carrying her pizza box in one hand and a manila envelope tucked under his arm. "You should really lock your door, Sophie." He paused in mid stride when he saw Sophie in the middle of her living room with her hand on Jack's chest.

Jack's eyes narrowed and his nostrils flared. Sophie could tell he was holding back his verbal bite. "Take all the time you need. Just don't expect me to be waiting when you're done." He cupped her cheek and pressed a punishing hot kiss to her lips. A kiss that contradicted what he'd just said. "Goodbye, Sophie."

His kiss left her breathless, and her heart shattered, the only evidence a single tear that worked a path down her face as she watched him storm by Marshall without saying a word. Jack slammed the door behind him and walked out of her life, leaving an empty void in his place. He left her, and only she was to blame.

"Bad timing?" Marshall asked.

"What are you doing here, Marshall?" Sophie's voice came out a whisper, all the fight in her gone. She swiped the tear from her cheek, hoping to hold everything together so Marshall wouldn't witness her tears. The anguish poked at her heart like a long, pointy spike ripping through to her soul.

Marshall hesitated while studying her a split second before he took charge with quiet assurance. After setting the pizza box and envelope down on the coffee table, he pulled her into his arms. He surrounded her with his strength and pressed a kiss into her hair. No words were exchanged. He just somehow knew. Uncontrollable sobs ripped free and her body shook.

"I'm so sorry, Sophie."

She didn't reply and just let his warmth surround her, hoping that he wouldn't ruin the moment by making a pass. She wasn't sure how much time had passed until her last tear fell, all of her energy drained. She left the security of his embrace and stepped back, not caring that her makeup was ruined, her eyes puffy, or that she was a mess.

"What are you doing here, Marshall?"

He picked up the envelope and handed it to her. "This is the information you wanted."

Her broken heart and zapped energy made the meaning of his words fuzzy. "I don't understand."

He rested his palm on her arm. "The envelope has the information on the person who hired us, along with information on Ryan." He kissed her temple. "Get some rest, Sophie."

Sophie held the envelope pressed to her chest. "That's it? You don't want to know what happened or anything?"

Marshall ran his hand through her hair, stroking the strands. He nudged a stray piece behind her ear. "Sophie...just get some rest." He pressed a single kiss to her forehead before stepping back and walking out. It wasn't that she wanted Marshall. Hell, it wasn't even that she didn't trust Jack to figure things out. Removing herself as an obstacle between them had been her only option. Now all she needed was her strength to hold out while she figured out the rest.

5 CHAPTER

Sophie kept her swollen red eyes hidden behind her sunglasses as she entered Dixon Security. Her sorrows had officially drowned around two in the morning from partaking in a bottle of tequila and the multiple bottles of wine Amber had brought over. Sophie's head pounded and her eyes hurt from the florescent lights. She stumbled into the gym, using her hand to steady herself against the wall. She inhaled a deep breath, hoping to hell that the training by her co-worker would kill her quickly. She'd asked for this ass-kicking. Hell, she'd even offered to pay for it. What had she been thinking?

Marshall stood in the middle of the mat, stretching as she entered the gym. Sophie dropped her bag onto the floor with the manila envelope sticking out of the top. She tossed her sunglasses on top of them before walking to the middle of the mat.

"Where's Aiden?"

"Tracking down a lead. You look like shit."

"Liquor will do that." She crossed her arms over her chest. "How did you know he was training me?"

His lips tilted up in a smile. "I didn't. Not until I came in this morning. Why didn't you tell me?"

Her shoulders deflated. She knew what he was doing, why he'd offered to step in. She wasn't an idiot. "Marshall, just because Jack and I are taking a break doesn't mean I'm fair game. I don't have the energy to play nice." She shook her head. "I think I'll just use the punching bag today, if that's okay."

She walked over to the punching bag and started to hit. There was no way she could handle the physical contact with Marshall today. She just wasn't ready.

He moved around to the other side of the bag, tilted his head from side to side stretching his neck before holding the bag still for her punches. "He loves you; you know that, right? He may not always say or do the right things, but he does love you."

Sophie put a little more effort behind her hit and her arm shook from the impact. "Yeah? He has a funny way of showing it."

Marshal's brows dipped to match his frown. "Why is that, because he wants to keep you safe? He offered me the one thing he cherishes most in his life, just to keep you safe. He was crushed when he saw the picture, and for a guy who doesn't let anything faze him, that says a lot. So tell me exactly what part of this don't you understand?"

Sophie dropped her hands to her sides. She didn't have the energy for a debate. She'd come in to work off her steam, not create more. The bag forgotten, Sophie paced back into the middle of the mat. "Marshall, before the serial killer and my abilities, I was lost and I was looking for my way. I've finally found a place where I fit in."—she pressed her lips together—"where I can actually do some good. Why can't he understand that?" She felt tears forming in her eyes. She swallowed around the large lump in her throat, fighting off the waterworks. "Why can't he just be happy for me?"

"Oh, Sophie..." Marshall whispered, stepping around the bag. "He's scared of losing you. He just doesn't know how to say it."

A tear fell free, leaving a wet path down her cheek. She swiped it away angrily before looking up and meeting his gaze. "You're not scared I'll get hurt. You believe in me. Why can't he?"

A flash of hesitation filled his eyes and he stepped back. "Sophie, don't do this...."

"Do what?" she asked, unsure of what he asked of her. Her gaze searched his for the answers.

"Don't make me fall in love with you too."

Laughter bubbled from her lips even as she shook her head. "I wouldn't dream of it. Now, come show me how to kick his ass so he'll quit worrying."

The door to the gym swung open. Jack stood in the doorway dressed in workout clothes. His gaze raked up her body and landed on her face. "If you're going to do this, you need to learn from the best."

Sophie crossed her arms over her chest. "Really? Is that supposed to be you?"

"It's both of us," Marshall whispered into her ear from right behind her. His fingers trailed a path down her arm.

Jack's gaze turned hungry as he approached like a predator ready to pounce. He stopped in front of her and leaned down, his breath hot on her neck. "We decided to share."

"You two don't know how to share." Her body trembled at his words. This wasn't happening.

Marshall leaned into the other side of her neck and pressed a kiss. "He's kidding, Sophie." He nibbled her ear lobe between his teeth. "Unless of course...that's what you want."

"How about a foursome?" Aiden asked from the door.

Her whole body flushed and her heart skipped a beat. "I'm afraid I can barely handle one of you...all three might put me in my grave."

"Like I always say, might as well go out with a bang." Aiden grinned as he winked. "Are you guys done torturing her yet? Because we have a problem."

Marshall stepped around her and placed his hand on her arm. "You two work this out. We'll be in the conference room when you're done."

"There's nothing to work out," she announced while trying to step around Jack. His warm palm stopped her retreat just as the gym door closed.

"Sophie, I can't promise not to worry about you."

Her head fell forward, her gaze on the blue mat.

"But I can promise that I love you and I'll do everything in my power to help you and to be the rock you need me to be."

She lifted her head and met his gaze. "Even if that means that I'll be working with Marshall?"

"Even then," he answered instantly. "I know you care about him, but I also know you love me, and I can't walk away from that. Not from you."

Sophie clasped her fingers around Jack's neck and pulled his mouth down to hers. "No more getting me fired."

His lips tilted up in a grin.

"No more thinking I'm screwing everyone I work with."

He winked.

"I need you in my corner, Jack. Will you be there for me?"

"I love you, Sophie," he announced, his voice husky before he pressed his mouth to hers in a kiss that was long overdue. He spread her lips with his tongue and tilted his head, deepening the connection she thought she'd never feel again.

His fingers caressed a path down to the small of her back, and his palm pressed against her, guiding her body closer to his. His erection pressed into the softness of her belly.

"Sorry to cut this short, but you guys need to hear this." Marshall's normally carefree tone now sounded worried and intense.

"We'll pick back up where we left off tonight?" he whispered into her ear, sending shivers down her spine. Anticipation stirred the butterflies awake in her belly.

She grabbed her gym bag from near the door, her fingers toying with the envelope sticking out of the top. Working last night after he'd left wasn't an option. His words had left her broken and battered, but today was a new day. Clasping her fingers with his, she walked by his side toward the conference room. Everything that mattered in her world was right again, back to normal. It was still a foreign place, a place she'd yet to feel comfortable. One day at a time, she reminded herself, knowing she couldn't rid the world of all evil.

Aiden was sitting across the room, facing the door. Marshall took his spot at the end of the table; and to Sophie's surprise, Ben was sitting next to Aiden. *Weekend worker? Ass kisser? Doesn't he have a life?* The IT guru's presence made her pause.

He clicked away at a laptop, not even noticing when they'd entered.

Sophie pulled out one of the chairs and sat, with Jack next to her, his fingers still locked with hers as if the mere touch would spark a memory she might have forgotten. Marshall glanced at Aiden. "You're up. What did you find out?"

Aiden stood up and starting pacing on his side of the table, his hands clasped behind his back, his brows furrowed in contemplation. "The woman killed last night outside the club was Macy Reyes."

The clicking stopped as Ben's fingers stilled on the keyboard, and his head popped up. "What did you say?"

"Macy Reyes was the woman killed," Aiden repeated while picking up a report from the table. "Twenty-five years old. She grew up in a little town in South Carolina called—"

"Covington." Marshall, Jack, and Ben all finished Aiden's sentence at the same time.

"Shit...I knew she looked familiar," Marshall exclaimed.

"None of us recognized her. The last time we saw her she was an awkward teen with short, cropped blonde hair."

Ben rubbed at his temples. "This isn't good, guys." He raised his head and met Marshall's gaze. "Who the hell hired you, and how come you didn't recognize the name?"

"I wasn't given the woman's fucking name, just a damn description." Marshall's tone held barely contained fury. "Had I known… Shit."

"Okay…" Sophie slid her fingers from Jack's and held up her palm. "Time out. What aren't you guys telling me? How do you know her?"

Sophie's gaze landed on each man in turn, waiting for one of them to tell her something that would help her comprehend the magnitude of what was going on. The silence in the room sliced through her like a knife in the back.

She shot out of her seat sending the chair flying back into the conference room wall. They were doing this again, keeping things and not trusting her. Hadn't they learned? Didn't they want her help? Anger surged through her, awaking every nerve in her body. "How do you expect me to help you if it's another secret like who Ryan is?"

Jack took Sophie's hand, trying to guide her into sitting back down, but she shrugged him off.

"She's his sister."

"Come again?"

"Macy was Ryan's little sister," Jack explained.

"Worse than that, she knew about the accident," Ben announced.

Jack and Marshall shared a silent look, communication without words or hand signals. The jerks.

"What accident?" Sophie asked.

"The one that killed Ryan." Ben held her gaze. "The same one Jack and Marshall were in." Ben whipped his gaze between the two guys. "You didn't tell her?"

"The information on the accident was in the envelope I gave her, the fact we were involved wasn't," Marshall announced through gritted teeth.

"Whoa...." She shook the confusion from her mind, her gaze whipping back and forth between the guys she thought she knew best. "You guys were in an accident, Ryan was killed, and the woman last night was his sister? Don't you think that was kind of important information to share?"

Sophie reached down and grabbed the envelope out of her bag. She tore open the flap and pulled the documents out. She sifted through the contents on Ryan. A watered-down version of the accident was there, but nowhere in the document did it say that either Marshall or Jack was involved.

She glanced up. "You weren't going to tell me you two were involved?"

Marshall remained silent.

"How come you guys aren't listed in the article?"

Jack and Marshall exchanged that look again. The one they used when contemplating censoring key information. Every time she saw that look, her blood boiled and she was ready to test out the new moves Aiden had taught her the day before.

"Ben, Aiden, can you guys give us a minute?" Marshall requested. The room remained quiet while she watched her co-workers leave.

The door had barely shut before she attacked. "Are you kidding me?" She walked around the table to stand behind the chair that Aiden had vacated, out of reach from both men, so she could look them in the eyes. "Start talking now, or I'm out….of everything."

Jack remained quiet, as if this was the moment he'd been dreading. He closed his eyes as if debating, but Marshall was the first to speak.

"We were seventeen and on the football team together."

Sophie remained quiet, watching Marshall find the courage to continue; only it wasn't Marshall who spoke next.

"We were damn good, too; the three best players Covington High ever had. We were headed to the championships and the sky was the limit after that." Jack's voice lowered. "But we were punks, and we thought we were invincible."

"But we weren't," Marshall added. "That night after the game we started celebrating early after dropping Macy at her friend's house to spend the night." Marshall's lips were tilted down in a frown. "We were such dumbasses."

"An animal ran out into the road," Jack added. "The alcohol slowed down Ryan's reaction time. He swerved, we rolled, and that was the last thing I remembered."

"I woke up first," Marshall declared. "I didn't know what to do, so I called the only person that I could think of."

She glanced between them both.

"The coach," Jack said, answering her unasked question. "Everything after that was a blur. He and the chief of police were brothers. Somehow he talked his brother into keeping our names out of the paper. Claimed no good would come of it, claimed we were just victims, and weren't the ones driving."

Sophie collapsed into the chair, letting the new information sink in.

"We didn't know until later that the vodka he was drinking was spiked with crushed-up pain medications."

"Who the hell did that, and why weren't you guys affected?"

Marshall shrugged. "We were drinking beer."

She shook her head, trying to make pieces of the facts they were feeding her. "Let's set aside the coach and the cops for now. If it was all hush-hush, then how does Ben know?"

"We were all shaken up and the two of us quit playing all together. Ben was on the team. He came looking to us for answers and we told him. He's kept our secret."

"Did the team go to the championship game without you two playing?"

They both shook their heads, their faces pressed into hard lines. This subject made them uncomfortable. The accident was a reminder that they weren't invincible.

"They didn't win another game the entire season when Mark didn't step in to play quarterback."

"Wait, who is Mark?"

"Mark is Sheriff Campbell's son. He was the second string.

"What happened to him? I would think that filling the role as a starter would be like a dream come true."

Jack shrugged. "His dad sent him away to live with his aunt; we weren't given a reason. He was just there one day and gone the next."

"Do you think he had anything to do with lacing the liquor with pain killers?"

"Nah, he was a good guy, a little weird around the edges, but I don't think he would have hurt anyone on the team."

Sophie leaned back in her chair with no more fight left in her.

"I can't imagine how you've lived with that your whole life. It would have eaten me up."

Jack leaned forward and clasped his fingers together. "No, Sophie, that accident did just the opposite. We still mourned our friend, but it made us want to be better men. We cleaned up our acts."

"We joined the Navy. They turned us into SEALs, and that gave us purpose. All of this time, we've watched out for his family. We send them money and talk to his mother at least once a month."

"You guys were just kids, and it's horrible that it happened, but if you kept up with his family, how did Macy end up here without you knowing who she was and who the hell killed her?"

"That's what we're going to find out," Marshall exclaimed.

Sophie pulled the paperwork closer and thumbed to the section that Marshall had included on who had hired Dixon Securities. She read through the application. "Says here that the person who hired you was Janice Miller. Who the hell is she?"

Jack's mouth parted and he swung his gaze to Marshall. He snapped his jaw shut and ground his teeth. "Are you fucking kidding me?"

Marshall shook his head and his look offered no apology. Another secret they weren't going to spill?

Jack lowered his head to rest in his palms. "Son of a bitch."

"Well?" Sophie asked. "Who is she?"

Marshall cleared his throat. "Jack, do you want to tell her, or do you want me to tell her?"

"I don't care who tells me. Just spill it already."

Jack lifted his gaze to hers, his eyes pleading, but for what she had no clue. "She was our girlfriend in high school."

"Okay, so you both dated her?"

Marshall cleared his throat again. "Yeah, us and half the team."

Jack let out a deep breath and leaned back in his chair. "Sophie, we both dated her at the same time, and worse than that, we knew we were seeing her simultaneously and used to joke about it."

"Oh, for the love of god." Sophie threw her hands up and rose. "So let me get this straight. Ryan drove drunk and died; his baby sister, Macy, was murdered, and the bitch you two were screwing in high school was the person who hired you for information?"

Sophie pressed her lips together in a fine line and shook her head. "I don't know you two at all, do I?"

That realization startled Sophie. The air around her grew thick and her breathing labored as she tried to digest this latest bit of information.

"I need some air." She grabbed her gym bag and walked to the door.

"It's worse than that," she heard Marshall say, effectively stopping her in her tracks.

She swiveled around to face them and adjusted the gym bag on her shoulder. "How?"

"She threatened to ruin Jack's career if I didn't help her get the intel she needed. She tried blackmail, claiming to have some damaging information that tied us to being in the car, even insinuating that we gave Ryan the liquor."

"Well, did you?"

The shared another look before Jack answered. "Back then, Vodka was my drink of choice. Ryan said he wanted to get wasted so I gave it to him and took his beer."

"So you were the target?"

He nodded. "I think so."

"You two are sinking fast. I guess it's time to really see what I'm made of."

With a newfound determination, Sophie pulled the door open. She stomped down the hallway to where Ben was sitting with Aiden and dropped her bag by the desk. "I need surveillance tape from the two hours prior to us showing up at the club until the time the police arrived. I want to know everyone who entered the premises, their names, and their faces, down to the employees. Can you do that?" She held Ben's gaze. When he didn't answer, she continued. "Or do I need to find someone else?"

Ben glanced over her shoulder before meeting her gaze. "If there was surveillance, I can hack it."

She nodded without looking over her shoulder. She knew they were both standing behind her. "Aiden, I need a complete workup on Janice Miller, who was raised in Covington. I need an address and I need to know her whereabouts, look locally. I think it's about time we all met. Can you call me on my cell?"

He kept his gaze on her without confirming with Jack or Marshall behind her. He nodded.

Sophie picked up her bag and headed down the hallway. "Where are you going?" Marshall called after her.

"I'm going to raise the dead."

6 CHAPTER

Sophie returned home and dropped her bag by the door. Her mind hadn't stopped thinking about the implications of what she'd learned. The fact that all of this was new information about the guy she'd been dating for months confused her the most. Hell, everyone had a past, good or bad; that was inevitable. She'd help them deal with this like they'd helped her solve the cold case when her abilities had just started to surface. She wasn't going down without a fight, even if she had to throw a few punches to get to the truth. Jack and Marshall needed her, and it was high time she returned the favor.

Sophie grabbed her yoga mat from the closet and unrolled it, setting it up on the floor. Meditation required a quiet mind, and right now that was an attribute she lacked. She sat down, crossed her legs, and closed her eyes. After each deep breath, she exhaled, imagining all of her stress floating away in a stream of energy from her body. She practiced meditation quite often, had even perfected her technique. Time seemed to stand still while she concentrated on her breathing and tried to push away all thoughts of her new life.

"Ryan," she called in her mind, hoping that the image of him would appear in her mind's eyes.

A glimpse of his face flashed on the black screen of the tiny looking television inside of her head, but his face faded just as quickly. She called him again, trying to concentrate on the electric energy from his soul. The same energy she'd felt in the white room.

His face flashed again, but it didn't stay.

"Have you figured out why he isn't showing up?" Sophie heard Will's voice in her ear. She refused to open her eyes and called for Ryan again. The same thing happened, without him appearing.

She let out an exasperated breath and pegged Will with a glare. Her guide sat next to her in full human form, as solid as any man currently in her life. "Obviously not, swami. Care to enlighten me?"

"He can't answer your question. It's your path to find the answers."

She pushed herself off the floor and placed her hand on her hip. "The master plan, right?" Exasperated, she threw her hands up, her reply laced with cold sarcasm. "I didn't cause their situation. Why can't I talk to him?"

"Figuring this little problem out is going to help you grow. Help you find your way."

"What good is it being able to talk to the dead when they're censored?" Her voice was hoarse with frustration. Her shoulders deflated. "Just give me a hint, one tiny hint."

He appeared in front of her. "Afraid not. This is all you."

Sophie narrowed her eyes and tried to hide her annoyance from the aggravating spirit she'd picked to guide her in life. "Remind me why I picked you again."

"Because you love me and trust that I will guide you where you need to be," Will answered matter-of-factly in his confident tone. The same tone that meant he wasn't about to give her the answers she needed.

"Don't be expecting that same feeling when I'm old and gray and we reunite the next time."

Will laughed. The deep, rich, silky sound was foreign to her ears, yet familiar at the same time. "Fine, one hint and that's all. The rest you have to figure out."

Sophie grinned as if she'd struck gold.

"To find your future, you have to trust your heart."

Will winked with a gleam in his eye before disappearing out of sight.

"That isn't a hint," she hollered to the ceiling. "I could have gotten that out of a fortune cookie."

Her door swung open and Amber strolled in carrying a carton from the bakery. "Fighting with Will again? If I didn't know any better, I'd think you two were married."

"He hates me."

"He's your guide."

"I'm pretty sure he just signed up for the job to torture me."

"Have some chocolate. It fixes everything." Amber opened the box and handed Sophie one of the cupcakes smothered in chocolate goodness.

Sophie licked the icing from her fingers and plopped down onto her couch. "How's Beau?"

"He's beautiful."

Sophie chuckled.

"Is he teaching you anything good?"

She wiggled her eyebrows. "Oh yeah."

"Besides new positions."

Amber grinned like she'd gotten caught stealing cookies from the cookie jar.

"Maybe."

Sophie debated dumping all of her worries on her best friend. Amber would know exactly the right thing to say to make light of the situation, but in the end, it wasn't really her story to tell, so she kept her mouth stuffed with cupcake and let Amber do most of the talking. Beau's eye color, the way he flirted with her, his rock-hard body, everything that best friends talk about, and yet Sophie couldn't help but let her mind wander to how her meeting was going to go with Janice, knowing the woman had slept with her boyfriend and her boss.

Sophie had just grabbed them both a soda from the fridge when she heard her cell phone ringing. She tossed everything out of the gym bag to get to it before it stopped.

"Masterson," she answered.

"You sound official," Aiden teased.

"I am official." Sophie grinned.

Aiden's voice lowered. "Listen, I found her, but the guys were breathing down my neck so they have the information too. If you want to beat them there, then I suggest you hurry to the motel. It's that sleazy place on I75 just outside of town. Room 125. I'll meet you there."

"I'm on my way," Sophie announced before ending the call.

She turned to find Amber already at the door. "Can I go with you?"

"Maybe after you let Beau teach you something that doesn't involve fighting sheets," Sophie teased as she grabbed her purse and keys.

Amber beamed a bright smile at Sophie. "Fine, but Soph….aren't you going to change? It's not like you to run around in yoga pants."

"Afraid I don't have time. Aiden's going to meet me there."

"Oh well." Amber waved her hand. "Aiden's waiting. Say no more. But what happened to Jack?"

"That kiss with Marshall happened to Jack, but we're working it out."

Sophie followed Amber out of her house and hopped in her car. She was closer to the motel than any of the guys were. It was ten minutes from her house versus the twenty to twenty-five minutes it was going to take them, depending on what type of head start Marshall and Jack had on her.

She pulled up in front of the motel and slowed as she drove down the strips of rooms, checking the room numbers as she went. She backed into the space across from the room and watched as the light inside flicked off. No one came out.

She grabbed her purse with the gun nestled inside and crossed the parking lot to the room. The door had been left open an inch. The room inside was dark and quiet. Sophie knocked, letting each one rap on the wood, and pushed the door a bit more open. When no one answered, Sophie gave it a little shove.

"I know you're in here. I saw you turn off the light," she announced, stepping into the darkened room with blackout window shades that covered everything but a slit at the top of the window. "I work for Dixon Security and I just need to ask you some questions. This won't take but a few minutes."

Sophie reached for the light switch and flicked it on before turning back toward the bed. A scream died in her throat as bile rose and her heart raced. A woman was sprawled on the bed, fully clothed with her legs and arms bound by rope, a bullet hole through the middle of her head. The pillow beneath was drenched in blood. She had a vacant look in her opened eyes. Sophie's gaze turned to the woman's ghostly presence standing next to the bed, looking down over her dead body.

The woman glanced up, her face confused. She whispered, "Look out."

Pain exploded in Sophie's temple, echoing behind her eyes and through her head. Her vision tunneled, caving in as if the blackness was attacking her. She closed her eyes, letting the darkness suck her under.

****

"This is the exact reason why you need to fire her. Damn it, Marshall," Jack yelled as he cradled Sophie's body against his chest. His quickened heart beat thumped against her ear.

"Calm down, Jack."

"How the hell do you expect me to calm down! That"—he pointed to the bed—"could be her. She isn't cut out for this shit, and you know it."

Jack took a deep, calming breath and pressed his lips to Sophie's forehead. He was scared. She couldn't blame him really. It was kind of sweet in a barbaric kind of way.

"If I didn't have a headache before, I have one now from all of the yelling," Sophie announced as she pushed to sit up.

Jack cupped her face. "We need to get you checked out."

She mustered up a reassuring smile. "I'm fine." She gave a slight nod. "Honest. I'm fine. The asshole caught me off guard and struck from behind."

"Sophie..." Marshall started.

Sophie stood on shaky feet and ignored the pain in her head. "Don't start, Marshall. I'm not a pansy and you aren't firing me. If it makes you feel better, I promise to wait for backup until I learn how to kick ass and I'm better prepared."

Marshall's brows dipped. "She had a momentary lapse of judgment, Jack. She'll be smarter next time, or I'll kick her ass."

"Next time she could be dead."

"Or not," Sophie replied.

"I hate to ruin the start of a good argument, but some of the finest from your precinct are pulling in. You may want to run interference so they don't shoot us," Aiden announced from the doorway.

Jack pulled Sophie close to his body and pressed a kiss into her hair. "Did you touch anything?"

She shook her head.

"Good, maybe they can lift prints."

****

An hour later, they were back at the precinct being held in separate interrogation rooms. Max was about to take Sophie's statement when the door opened. A brunette woman wearing a pencil skirt and blazer walked in, carrying a black leather briefcase. The resemblance between this woman and Aiden was uncanny. Same cheekbones, same color hair, and like Aiden, this woman looked as if she was ready to kill but in a completely different way. Somehow Sophie knew this woman was related to her teammate and also knew she was just as lethal.

"Miss Masterson?" she asked.

"Yes." Sophie tried to hide the uncertainty from her voice.

"I'm your attorney, Alexis Monroe." She handed her card to Max. "Unless you have evidence implicating my client or charges to press, we're through here."

Max turned his gaze to Sophie and he looked just as confused as she felt. "You do realize who she is?" Max asked Alexis.

"I'm very familiar with who she is. She's your sister, which is another reason why you shouldn't be the one questioning her to begin with." Alexis tilted her head as if tired of the conversation. "Let's go, Sophie. Have a good day, Chief."

Sophie rose, unsure if she could really leave. She followed the attorney to the door, only stopping to pat her brother on the chest. "We'll talk later."

"I advise against that, Miss Masterson," Alexis announced, taking Sophie by the elbow and leading her out of the office.

"Did Marshall ask you to come?"

The attorney shook her head but kept walking. "We'll discuss it in the car."

Sophie jogged down the steps of the police station and paused. A limo, complete with driver, was parked in front. "Who are you?"

Alexis turned and let out a lengthy sigh. "Do we have to do this now?"

The limo driver held the door open, waiting.

"Lady, I'm not going anywhere with you until you tell me who you are."

"Listen here, you little twit." The woman took a step closer into Sophie's face. "If it were up to me, I'd let you rot in jail. Luckily for you, it's not up to me. I owed a favor and now it's paid."

Sophie balled her fingers into a fist. Blood boiled in her veins as she sought to reel her inner bitch back under control. "I don't even know you, lady, but call me twit one more time and we'll see which bitch is left standing."

Alexis's cheeks reddened. The air between them was electric. Sophie was going to have a knock-down, drag-out fight right in front of the police station. She was going to jail all right, but not for murder...for assault.

"You might have all of these guys fooled but not me."

"What the hell is your problem? I don't even know you."

Alexis stepped closer, her fingers balled into a fist, and Sophie watched Alexis pull a mask of calm back over her face. Her angry lines smoothed and she gave Sophie a shit-eating smile.

Aiden stepped out of the limo. "Alexis, you don't want to do that. I'm training her, and she can kick your ass. "

Alexis looked down her nose at Sophie judgingly as she swept her gaze up and down her body. "I don't know what all of you see in her."

Alexis was the first to slide into the limo as Aiden tossed his arm over Sophie's shoulders. "You'll have to forgive my sister. She's kind of territorial."

"Whose territory is she protecting?" Sophie asked and Aiden ignored her, ushering them both into the back of the limo.

Alexis opened a bottle of water and poured the clear liquid into a crystal glass before taking a sip and ignoring them both.

Sophie took her time sizing up the venomous woman and then glanced back and forth between Aiden and Alexis. "Twins?"

"Triplets," Aiden answered. "We may look alike, but the similarities stop there."

"Yeah, I can see that." Sophie grinned. "You don't have a stick up your ass."

Aiden's chuckle resonated through the back of the limo as Sophie held Alexis's perturbed stare. Alexis wouldn't win this pissing match. Her red-painted lips were pressed into a fine line. "I'm not here to be your friend, Miss Masterson. I'm here as your legal counsel."

"I don't recall asking for either."

Aiden leaned forward, resting his elbows on his knees. "Okay, everyone needs a time out. Alexis, you'll represent her if she needs you, and, Sophie...try to play nice. Alexis is doing me a favor. You were at the scene of a crime where a murder had been committed. We found you passed out. I know you didn't do it, but until they have the evidence that shows you didn't do it, I thought you might need a little help."

She let his explanation sink in.

"What about Marshall and Jack? Did you spring them too?"

Alexis answered that one. "No. Depending on the time of death, they have an alibi; they all arrived at the same time. You were the only one in the room when they got there."

She crossed her arms over her chest. "That's not true."

Alexis's lips tilted up at the corner. "Really? Do you care to enlighten us?"

"The killer, the same guy who struck me, was in the room." She lifted her hand to her temple and rubbed the tender spot. "Where do you think I got this?"

"Easily staged," Alexis suggested.

Sophie lunged for the lawyer's throat just as Aiden's arm fastened around her waist, pulling her back to sit on his lap.

"She has anger issues," Alexis announced.

"The only issue I have is with the bitch sitting across from me," Sophie corrected.

"Be that as it may, I'm still the bitch that kept you out of jail, as much as it pained me to do it."

Alexis placed the glass in the holder and crossed her legs. Aiden's grip held firm on Sophie's hips. Was he expecting her to jump again? Of course he was.

"Let's get one thing straight, Miss Masterson."

Sophie smiled, but it was a smile filled with venom; she was ready to strike. "Great idea, Counselor."

"You are nothing more than a favor to my brother who felt pity for you, but if you think that all you have to do is open your thighs to get a man like Marshall Dixon into your bed, you're wrong. He'll see right through to the floozy that you are."

"Aw....does someone have their panties in a bunch?"

All the tension eased from Sophie's body. This was about Marshall? How and when did that happen?

The limo pulled up outside of a four-story law office building downtown. The marque read Monroe and Monroe, Attorneys at Law. Just peachy perfect.

Alexis slid out of the limo, not bothering to say goodbye. The driver shut the door and left Sophie and Aiden alone in the back.

"Why doesn't that sign say Monroe times three? Was law not your thing?" Sophie asked, looking at Aiden with new eyes.

"Really? You're going to lead with that question? You don't want to know what she meant about Marshall?"

Sophie grinned and moved to the seat across from Aiden to look him in the eyes. She grabbed two bottled water from the mini fridge and tossed one to him. She took a sip and relaxed back into her seat, letting the cool water soothe her throat.

Aiden's eyes twinkled with mischief. "Been there, done that. I got the degree and T-shirt and was bored."

Sophie's mouth parted. She hadn't expected that answer. "Not enough danger?"

Aiden chuckled. "Not enough sexy women." He winked. "Think about it, the only women who come in that place are married and looking for a divorce, or about to get married and wanting a pre-nup, or they were arrested for some other crime and are looking for representation. What makes you think any of those women would interest me?"

"I'm sure there are more women than that. Think of all the interns you could have chased."

"Women like dangerous men."

"Women also like smart men," she countered.

"Are you saying you like me, Sophie?"

She shook her head. "I've already told you, Aiden; we're friends. I have enough men in my life." She gave him an apologetic smile. "So now what happened between Marshall and your sister?"

"You happened to Marshall."

"I'm dating Jack. Or rather....was dating Jack. It's still up in the air. I didn't lead Marshall on."

"Sophie...you didn't have to. And don't take this the wrong way, but you have a certain appeal that just begs men to notice. Take me for example. I noticed before you even spoke a word."

"You were horny."

"That too. But the more I know you, the more I understand the attraction. You're kind, you have a big heart, and you're not afraid to stand up for what you believe in. It doesn't hurt that you've got a body that men just want to grab and your lips....let's not forget your lips." Aiden shivered. "All that aside, let me give you a piece of advice."

That got Sophie's attention. "More advice from the playboy?"

"Figure out what you want and decide for yourself. You have to live with your decision."

"And they don't?"

"Sophie, do I have to teach you everything?"

"Apparently."

"I've worked with Marshall for a long time. The fact that he's stepping back and letting you and Jack figure things out says volumes about the type of guy he is. Start paying attention, woman."

Paying attention. She thought she had been. She turned her gaze toward the window and watched the passing scenery until they came upon the motel where she'd left her car. Crime scene tape covered the room. White powder residue was left on the windows. Sophie's heart broke for the woman who had died inside. She was the only apparition to try and warn Sophie that she was about to be attacked. She didn't deserve her fate, and Sophie was going to do everything in her power to bring the bastard who'd done this to her to justice.

Aiden grabbed his backpack, unzipped it, pulled out Sophie's purse and handed it to her. "I didn't want you to lose this, so I grabbed it when we found you."

"Taking evidence from the scene of a crime is illegal."

He grinned. "I know a great lawyer. Besides, I didn't want the cops to think that the gun inside was the one used to kill her. It wasn't, was it?"

Sophie chuckled. "No, Aiden, it wasn't. I'm saving my bullets for the bastard that is doing this to Jack and Marshall."

Aiden did a slight shiver and grinned. "I love it when your kitten shows her claws. It's so hot."

"Take a cold shower and meet me at the office in the morning. We've got a killer to find."

Sophie pulled up outside her apartment and hurried up the sidewalk toward her front door. Her nosey neighbor, Gladys, was sitting on the stoop.

"You should have told me the cable guy was coming today," the old woman crooned. "I would have scheduled him to look at my box too."

Sophie paused in her tracks; her gaze flew back to her front door as she clutched her purse tighter to her chest. "Did he go inside?"

The old woman nodded. "Yeah, he did, and he made a racket while he was in there. You must have had some major rewiring going on."

Shit and double damn. This didn't bode well. "Did you get a good look at him?"

The woman grinned. "As much as I could. He kept his hat pulled down so I didn't get a good look at his face, but he had a nice body."

"Did you notice the name of the company on the van?"

"Yes, dear. It was our local provider's van. Are you all right?" Concern laced her voice.

"I didn't have a cable guy scheduled for today. I didn't have one at all."

7 CHAPTER

Sophie dug the phone out of her pocket and called the police station. "Hey, Velma, this is Sophie. Can you tell me if any of the cable company vans were called in as stolen?"

"Hey, Soph, let me check."

"Thanks." Hold music crooned through the speaker until there was a click.

"As a matter of fact, there was one reported a couple of hours ago. Did you see it?"

"No, but I'll keep my eye out. Thanks."

Sophie disconnected the phone and dropped to her knees next to the old woman's chair. Did this constitute waiting for backup? She pressed her lips together, remaining motionless while she decided what to do next. Crap.

She dialed Jack's number. His voice mail clicked on, telling her to leave a message. She hesitated, not wanting to leave a message that would make him worry. "Hey, Jack. Can you call me when you get this? I might have a situation."

She hung up and dialed Marshall. "Hey, Sophie, are you okay? My attorney said that you were released."

"Yeah, Aiden called in a favor and his sister bailed me out."

There was a pause on his end of the line. She considered teasing him, maybe putting him on the spot, or asking embarrassing questions, but decided against all three. She had more important matters than to press him about his love life.

"Hey listen; you know how you told me to call for backup? Would unauthorized entry into my house qualify as one of those times?"

"Where are you?" His voice was tense and she could imagine the look in his eyes.

"At my place. Well, actually outside. I apparently had a visit from the cable company today, only I didn't call anything in. They went inside."

"Do you have your gun?"

Sophie pulled open the purse and checked inside to make sure it was still there, not trusting that the little bitch of a lawyer didn't have access to her purse to replace the gun with something un-useful like a paperweight. "Yes."

"I'll be there in ten minutes. Do. Not. Go. In. Do you hear me?"

"Sir, yes, sir," she teased.

Within ten minutes, Marshall, Aiden, Roman, Beau, and Dash had her street blocked with various vehicles. The neighbors that were home were out on their lawns and stoops, none brave enough to come ask her what was going on.

"Oh my," her neighbor, Gladys, exclaimed, lifting her hand to her chest. "Aren't they something?"

"That was my first reaction too," Sophie teased, standing next to her neighbor's chair, where she'd been waiting patiently for them to show. Marshall headed toward her, took the keys out of her hand, and tossed them to Roman, who was already at her door with his gun drawn.

"You okay?"

She smiled. "Yeah, I'm sorry. I didn't know who else to call. I'm sure the guy is long gone by now."

"Sophie, he could have left a bomb inside, or worse. You did the right thing." Marshall scanned the parking lot in front of the townhouses before heading toward her front door.

"Hey, Marsh?" she called after him.

He turned at the threshold. "Yeah?"

"I'm just curious, what would be worse than a bomb?"

His lips slimmed into a thin line. "You don't want to know."

He disappeared inside with the others and she paced the front lawn.

Her neighbor momentarily went inside her house and returned with a bowl of popcorn before

93

retaking her seat in the lawn chair. "You should invite them over more often. This is better than my soap operas."

Sophie swung her gaze to the old bat. "I guess you'd like a little notice next time too, so you can call over all of your bingo buddies?"

Gladys grinned. "Not all of them, just a select few. Some of them have heart pacers and couldn't handle the view."

Sophie gave a slow nod of understanding.

Sophie waited for the time to tick by as if she were waiting for water to boil. Time seemed to stand still. Marshall wasn't gone ten minutes and yet she was ready to go find him. Biting down on her nail, Sophie breathed a sigh of relief when Marshall finally resurfaced, carrying her overnight bag with him.

"Wh...."

He shook his head. "I'll explain in the car." He pulled out a card and handed to the Gladys, who was watching the free show of hot men parading in and out of Sophie's house. "Please let me know if anyone else goes into Sophie's house when she's not home. There is a reward involved."

The old woman's eyes lit up at the word. She slid the card from his fingers and shoved in inside her bra. "Sure thing, handsome."

Aiden stepped out of the apartment; instead of throwing her a one liner or teasing her about a vibrator he'd found, his face was pressed into hard lines. "Marshall, every bit of it is compromised. It's going to take a while for us to go through it all."

He gave a slight nod. "Call in your teams if need be. Let's get this done tonight. Replace everything that isn't salvageable."

Sophie's mouth parted, her heart sinking like concrete into her stomach. "What does that mean?"

He guided her by the elbow, not stopping to explain while he led her to the car. His long, sure strides quickened, making her double her steps to keep up. He opened the door, impatiently waiting for her to get in. "I'll tell you about it after we leave."

Marshall rounded the car and got in the driver's side. She'd seen the anger in his eyes, his brow creased with worry.

"Tell me what you found."

He turned on the ignition and tossed it into gear. His grip on the steering wheel tightened, turning his knuckles white.

"Video feed, Sophie. We found video feed throughout your entire house. There was no part left untouched."

Her mouth fell open and her mood veered sharp and fast from confusion to anger. "Surely not the..."

"Yes. Two in the bathroom, one directly into the shower, your bedroom...the whole house was infested with them."

"Where does the feed lead?" she asked in a calm and steady voice, a direct contrast to the venom coursing in her veins.

Marshall slid his fingers through hers and squeezed her hand. The reassuring gesture did little to quench her thirst for blood from the asshole who had gone through her things. What if she'd still been there or, worse, if Amber had been there?

"We don't know yet."

"Thank god for my nosey neighbor," Sophie whispered while leaning back into the leather seat. Someone was watching her. Well, someone had planned to anyway.

She turned to Marshall with a fresh idea in mind. "What if we use it against him? Whoever it is obviously wants to know my every move. So let's leave a trail of bread crumbs right to us."

"Sophie, he's probably already watching them dismantle the feed."

Her shoulders deflated, all hope for retribution immediately dashed. "Then he knows we're on to him. Just means we need to find him quicker."

Marshall released her hand and she missed his warmth and heat. His touch and presence grounded her, lending her an invisible strength she needed. Everything Alexis had said came rushing back to her. "Marshall, this guy is obviously from your past. You know what this means, right? It's someone who knew about the accident. We're going to have to go to Covington and see what we can dig up."

He pressed his lips together. "Sophie, you know Jack and I aren't the same guys from back then. We've changed."

Sophie placed her palm on Marshall's arm and quickly regretted it. She felt the hard, corded muscles beneath her palm. "Learning from our mistakes makes us who we are. I won't think any differently of Jack or you, no matter what we find."

He didn't look reassured. His gaze remained focused as he continued down the road.

"Which hotel are you taking me to?"

He shook his head. "You're not going to a hotel, and you're definitely not going back to Jack's after what happened last time. You're coming to my house."

"You really don't—"

"It's not up for debate, Sophie. It's my house or one of the other's, if you'd feel more comfortable with them. This guy gained access to your home, and there's no telling if this is the first time or if he's already been there before; so until this is over, you're staying with one of us."

"Okay." She didn't argue. She wasn't stupid. She knew she needed help. "So who are you sending to Covington with me? I couldn't reach Jack, so I don't know if he'll be able to leave on a moment's notice or not."

"We'll work it out. Don't worry about it tonight."

****

An hour later, and safely behind the big iron gates that surrounded Marshall's house, Sophie and Marshall each had a slice of meat lover's pizza sitting in front of them. He grabbed two beers from the fridge and handed her one.

"You know what I don't get?"

"What's that?" Marshall asked, pulling a string of cheese away from his mouth.

"If this is about the accident, why is this guy killing everyone involved or who might know? I mean, wouldn't he want to make it public to at least embarrass you guys? He'd need people to corroborate his story. What he's doing doesn't make sense."

"Sophie, if I had to guess, this guy isn't thinking at all."

She shoved her hair behind her ears. "Really? He's killed two people, knocked me over the head, wired my house, and let's not forget that he sent the picture to break up me and Jack." She picked up her dish and took it into the sink before hopping up on the countertop and letting her feet dangle over the side. "This guy is screwing with your lives. It has to be personal."

Marshall stood and took care of his dish and then walked over to her, standing between her legs. His warm palms rested on her hips. "Is it over?"

"Is what over?"

His gaze lingered on her lips, causing her mouth to go dry before it caressed a path up her face to reach her eyes. "You and Jack."

Her body gravitated toward his, yet she caught herself before giving in to the temptation. Her heart raced just as quickly as her mind. She shrugged and swiped her tongue across her parched lips. "Marshall...I don't know what we are. We were going to talk about it tonight, but when I tried to call him before you, I couldn't reach him."

Marshall's lips were a mere inch from hers. She saw the hesitation in his eyes; it matched her own.

"Why did you break up with Alexis?" Her voice came out a whisper, pulling him from his thoughts.

He cupped her cheek, and the lines of his face softened. "Because of you. I promised I wouldn't lie to you. I broke up with her because of you."

Sophie leaned into his hand, letting his warmth soak into her cheek. Would he kiss her again? Did she want him to? Would it be the same as it had been in the club? His warmth surrounded her, drawing her to him like something she craved. Something she needed. She calmed her desires, ignoring the carnal demands. "I was with Jack. I mean...I'm still with Jack. She's."—Sophie swallowed around her dry throat—"very pretty."

Marshall's lips quirked up in a grin. "She doesn't hold a candle to you." Marshall let his hand drop and stepped back out of her space. Clearing his throat, he held out his hand to help her off the counter, but she bypassed it knowing if she were to touch him they might end up doing something they'd both regret. She jumped down of her own accord.

His lips twitched. "You'll be staying in the room across from mine, unless of course you care to share the same bed."

"Spare room is fine," she answered, the high pitch of her voice giving away her unease. "Maybe we should call Jack and tell him what's going on."

"Jack, right," Marshall replied as he pushed open the door to the spare room and waited for her to enter. "Why don't you go ahead and soak in the tub, and I'll bring in your bag. I'm sure your muscles could use the break, especially after the day you've had. I'll try and call Jack when you get out."

Sophie stepped into a room larger than her entire apartment. It was as if she'd stepped into a magazine. The elegant design and matching colors hinted that a decorator had created the space.

Marshall sidestepped her and moved farther into the room, opening one of the other doors. "The bathroom is fully stocked with towels and everything you'll need, so make yourself at home."

Sophie stepped into the bathroom with a Jacuzzi style tub, and she felt the tension easing from her body just from knowing what relief waited ahead for her.

"Just come out when you're ready."

"I may never come out." She turned in place.

Marshall chuckled. "You will if you don't want me to come in and check on you. Let me know if you need help washing your back."

Sophie heated at the thought. Embarrassment seeped into her body. She shouldn't want that. She shouldn't want him, not when things were hanging in the balance with Jack. "I think I can manage."

"Your bag will be on the bed, and if there's anything I've forgotten to pack, we can pick it up tomorrow."

"Marshall…"

"Yes, Sophie." He was at the bathroom door with his hand on the knob when he turned around.

"You've never pretended with me, so let me be straight with you."

His brow cocked, his look expectant.

"Right or wrong, I feel the pull between us too. There's just too much…" Her head dropped forward as she tried to find the right words.

He closed the distance between them, using his finger to lift her chin so she would meet his gaze. "I get it." His green eyes captivated her, drawing her in like a light illuminating her way home. "I will never pressure you, and right now…you aren't in the right frame of mind to decide."

Sophie swallowed around the lump in her throat and stifled the words that would deny what he'd said. She didn't have a response for that. He was right.

He cupped her cheek, his eyes searching hers. "Make no mistake. I want you to pick me. I want to be the man you wake up with every morning. The man who you look forward to seeing every night. I want intimate talks and stolen kisses. I want you, Sophie. I want it all, but I know you can't give it to me yet, and I respect you for that."

He pressed a kiss to her temple. His lips lingered against her skin. She closed her eyes. Every fiber of her wanted him, needed him, and yet, there was Jack.

Sophie's eyes slid open when his warmth disappeared. She stood rooted in place as she watched him walk out of the bathroom. The quiet click of the door closing filled the room and she let out a breath she didn't realize she'd been holding.

****

Marshall closed the door to the bedroom and leaned back against the wood. It had taken all of his resolve not to kiss her, not to take her where she stood. He hadn't been lying when he said he wanted more. He did, and he wouldn't have screwed up being with her over one single kiss. He'd learned his lesson in the club. She was sweet and hot and melted into his arms. She wouldn't resist, but he refused to take the decision away from her. She needed to realize the same thing he already knew, if they were ever going to be together.

He tried to push the thoughts out of his head as he walked into his bedroom and took a cold shower. Her being close enough to touch, yet so far away in her mind and heart, he had needed to steel his nerves, drawing on every reserve of willpower not to go back to her. Marshall hurried through his cold shower and slid into some track pants after stepping out. He ran a towel over his face and hair and tossed it in the hamper before heading into his office.

He was booting up the computer when his phone rang. "Dixon."

"I didn't want you to shoot me when I walked in, but I'm pulling into your driveway," Jack said into the phone.

"You know the code. Let yourself in. I'm in the office," Marshall replied before the line went dead.

Marshall opened an email that Ben had sent him an hour ago. The message was short and to the point.

I pulled up the surveillance Sophie wanted from the club and decided to check the entire day instead of those couple of hours. I found some footage from around late morning, before you guys ever showed up on the scene. I think you need to see this before Sophie.

Marshall clicked the link and made the picture bigger. He stared in horror as he saw his best friend, Jack Love, standing with his back against the building of the club, his hands firmly planted on Janice Miller's hips. The same woman that both he and Jack had shared in high school. They were in a heated discussion, yet there was no sound. She tried to pull away and he pulled her back. One hand landed on her hip while she used the other to gesture. Her open palm landed as a smack on his face. He grabbed her hand and she wrestled, using her other hand to loosen his hold. Her nails dug into his wrist as she twisted her arm free. Jack held a momentary look of shock and anger, his reaction quick. He reached for her and drew her near. He cupped the back of her neck, whispered a few words, and then he leaned down and pressed his lips to hers in a kiss that lasted for more than a few seconds.

"Oh shit," was Marshall's only reply as he plopped down in the chair.

Jack strolled into Marshall's office. "Where's Sophie? I stopped by her house, and the guys told me what happened and that she's with you."

Marshall rose out of his chair and advanced on Jack so quickly he didn't know what hit him. He pinned his best friend up against the wall. Anger welled in his chest.

"How could you do that to her?" Marshall asked through gritted teeth.

Jack shoved against Marshall's chest, pushing him away. "What the hell are you talking about?"

Marshall stalked over to the desk and swung the monitor around to face Jack and pressed play.

"This, you fucking bastard. How could you do this to Sophie!" He pointed at the screen, watching the entire scene over again. "Have you lost your fucking mind?"

He heard Sophie's breath hitch and spun toward the hallway. Her hand was over her mouth, her face was white, and her look was stricken as she silently watched the video. Jack spun around yet remained silent. Marshall pinched the bridge of his nose. "Sophie, you weren't supposed to see that."

Her palm was on her stomach, but the color was slowly returning back to her face.

"I can explain," Jack said and held out his hand to her.

She stomped over to him and lifted his hand, turning to his inner wrist to verify the scratch marks were there. Seconds later, she dropped it as if it was about to burn her. She stepped around him, walking farther into the room and over to the crystal decanter of liquor on the bar in the corner. She lifted the lid and grabbed a glass. Her hand shook as she held the bottle, first pouring a couple of fingers of the amber liquid and draining it before pouring another one. She took several deep breaths upon finishing.

"It's no different than what you did with Marshall," Jack started to say.

She spun around to face him and took a deep breath. "So she was your job?"

Sophie's cheeks grew redder the longer she waited for a response, a response that they all knew she wasn't going to like.

"She told me she had proof from the accident. She threatened to pin the drugged vodka on us.

She said that she knew the pills came from my house and implied we were both in on it."

"Were the pills from your house?"

Jack glanced down at his feet. "My mom had a prescription and accused me of taking some." He looked up to hold her gaze. "But I didn't, I swear it. Janice said she was going to make it public if I didn't give her what she wanted."

"I think it's pretty clear what she wanted." Sophie held up her hand and shook her head.

"It's not like that, Sophie."

Sophie looked up at the ceiling and closed her eyes before meeting his gaze. "Fine...then tell me what she wanted." Sophie tilted her head. "I'm listening."

Jack lowered his gaze once more, unable to look Sophie in the eye, and Marshall knew the answer wasn't going to be good.

"Tell me, damn it. What the hell did she want?" Sophie demanded when Jack didn't answer.

"She wanted me back," he answered while lifting his gaze to meet Sophie's. "I told her no, and she hit me."

Sophie folded her arms across her body. "So you drove home your point with a kiss?"

"I panicked. When I told her no, she threatened Marshall's and my career. I had to calm her down. I swear that was all it was." Jack took a step in her direction, but she rounded the desk out of his reach.

"How come you didn't tell us when Marshall told us who hired him?" she asked. "Or at the motel? How come you didn't say anything?"

"It was a mistake. I didn't want to lose you. It was no different than you kissing Marshall."

She shook her head. "Jack, I told you that night we needed to talk. I had every intention of telling you. I wasn't keeping it a secret. You, on the other hand, I don't believe you would have ever told me the truth without the footage surfacing."

"Speaking of the video and the picture..." Marshall chose that moment to interrupt. "Someone is still out there trying to ruin us." He glanced at Jack. "Both of us. I don't know about you two, but I damn sure want to find out who it is."

Sophie let out a long breath and turned to Marshall. "I'm on the next flight out to Covington." She pegged them both with a look that dared them to disagree. "Alone."

"You'll take the company jet." He nodded, already knowing where the next step would lead them. She wasn't going alone. She didn't know that yet, but he did. "So you think a bunch of strangers are going to open up to you about the accident?"

She narrowed her eyes. "Well if you two didn't spike the vodka, someone sure as hell did and I think it's time to go shake things up."

"Great. I'll be ready to go in the morning," Jack announced."

She spun around and shook her head. "I'll manage without you."

Jack's gaze turned pleading. "Sophie, don't leave me like this. We need to talk."

She shook her head. "I don't think there's anything left to say." She walked out of the office, leaving Marshall to deal with the aftermath.

Jack plopped down in one of the chairs. "You've got to be eating this up. She's all yours now."

Marshall poured them both a drink and handed Jack a glass. "You screwed up, Jack." Marshall sipped his drink and let the burn go down his throat. "And for the record, she isn't mine. She's always kept me at arm's length because of you. Dude..." Marshall shook his head.

"I know. You don't have to tell me. I know..."

Marshall stayed in his office, lost in thought long after Jack left. Getting his friend to leave had been hard. Promising not to make a move on Sophie until they figured out who was behind the setups was even harder. Yet he agreed out of nothing other than his friendship with Jack. They were all in a crappy predicament. There was no way for them to all walk away from this happy. It was inevitable. Someone was going to be heartbroken when it was all said and done. Marshall rested his head in his hands and rubbed at his temples. His headache prickled just behind his closed lids.

****

"There's only one thing I don't understand," Sophie announced while leaning against the doorframe of Marshall's office. Her voice sounded quiet in the darkened room where Marshall had his head in his palms.

He looked up and his gaze met hers. "Only one?"

Sophie wrapped her arms around her midsection. Her gaze strayed to the computer monitor where she'd watched the video of her boyfriend holding another woman in his arms. Sophie pushed the thought out of her head, not ready to deal with the implications. She stepped into the office and sat down in one of the plush leather chairs. "Who has the most to gain or want revenge?" She chewed her bottom lip for a second before she continued. "If you think about it in terms of motive and wanting to get a step ahead of the killer, what is the likely motive, and what do you think he'll do next?"

Marshall's brow rose as he leaned back into his chair. Resting his elbows on the armrests, he steepled his fingers in front of him. "Motive is the unknown. If we knew that, then we would know who it is. The next step should be easier to figure out."

Sophie tilted her head. "What's that?"

"The person is obviously trying to set up me and Jack and using the incident and people from our past. That's the given; that's the easy part, but what I don't think you've realized yet….is the next logical step."

"Assuming the killer is logical."

Marshall nodded. "Assuming that he is, what do you think he'll do next?" he asked as if quizzing her.

She leaned back in her chair. "That depends. I think we're all looking at this the wrong way. You're assuming"—she used air quotes around the word—"that this guy is out to destroy you. If that were the case and he had the evidence, then why not just take it public and hit you both where it counts…in your reputation? I mean think about it, it would kill both Jack's career and your future business. I guess that's why I think this is more personal. It's not just about righting a wrong; it's about making you both suffer and go crazy, knowing neither of you could do anything to stop it. What could make a man or woman that hell bent on destruction that they would kill people just to get into your heads?"

"I don't know."

Sophie shrugged, and as much as she tried to deny it, she knew who would be next. She was the common thread between the two, just like the women who'd been killed. Her time was coming, and if she was right, the clock had already started ticking. Sophie sat back and regarded Marshall. He was a beautiful man, completely out of Sophie's league, not to mention her boss. Why he even cared about her she wouldn't ever understand.

"You do realize I'm a target." She announced it as a statement and not a question.

"I do."

"I'm not going into hiding."

Marshall's lips tilted up at the corners. "I never thought you would."

"Good."

Marshall cleared his throat. "About Jack…"

She held up her palm and stood. "Let's not."

"We should."

She shook her head and started for the door. "No, we shouldn't."

"It's inevitable."

She couldn't think of a good enough comeback. She glanced back over her shoulder. "Good-night, Marshall."

Sophie left the office. Her retreat was all she needed, well, that and distance while her head, heart, and body warred with different opinions on which man she should take. As if taking either of them was what she needed to keep her sanity intact.

8 CHAPTER

Sanity, Sophie thought while adjusting her seatbelt firmly across her lap. She gave a nice tug on the tongue, ensuring she'd stay seated for the flight. The roar of the plane's engines vibrated through the small aircraft as it started down the runway. Her stomach twisted in knots from the anticipation. She gripped the armrest with tight fingers and stilled her nerves.

"Relax," the man sitting next to her suggested.

She glanced at one of the men she'd chosen for this trip. One of the men who not only didn't have a vested interest in the outcome of catching the killer but wasn't a threat to her heart. She gave a tight-lipped smile to Aiden. "I'll relax when we land."

Across the table from her, the clicking on the keyboard stopped, and then Ben shut the computer down. "The pilot has twenty-two years' experience. I've personally checked his credentials and should anything happen while in the air..." Ben grinned. "Aiden here can fly the plane. You have nothing to fear, Sophie."

Relaxing was an option she didn't have. As far as nothing to fear, maybe not in the air or on the plane, but when they landed, it would be a completely different story.

She eased her death grip on the leather seat and inhaled a deep breath. She'd briefly closed her eyes, her mind set on meditation, but the first jolt from turbulence made her eyes pop open.

"How did you do it?" Aiden asked, grabbing his drink sitting on the table between them and Ben.

"Do what?"

"Get both of them to stay behind. I'm impressed," Aiden announced with a twinkle in his eye. The guy probably thought he might get lucky.

"They had no choice. I wasn't bringing them and they didn't want me to go alone. I was going regardless. I'm just letting you two tag along for good measure."

"Why us? Why not Dash or Beau or even Roman? You're secretly crushing on me, aren't you?"

Sophie rolled her eyes, unable to help it. "I brought Ben for his contacts and to get the locals to open up, not to mention his computer 'techniques' should they not cooperate, and you....you're my muscle. It's the least you can do since you bailed on me at our last lesson. You fed me to the sharks, offering me up on a silver platter. You deserve a nice trip down memory lane." She shrugged. "It doesn't hurt that you're an attorney."

"Feeling particularly dramatic today, are we, sweetheart?" Aiden grinned. "I'm not a practicing attorney, and I'm sure you don't want me calling my sister in to save us."

A shiver skirted down Sophie's spine. The thought of Alexis lifting a finger in Sophie's business had her gritting her teeth against the idea.

"They don't know you aren't practicing. If nothing else, you know the law, and that's what we're dealing with, lawmen who, from the sounds of it, could use a good course on ethics."

You're running, Will announced in her mind.

She shook her head against the thought and closed her eyes. *Go away. I'm not running. I'm jumping into the fight feet first.*

The fight isn't what I'm talking about, and you know it. I'm referring to following your heart.

A bandage can't mend the crack. I refuse to hurt them or let anyone hurt me again. It's not going to happen.

Just because one man hurt you doesn't mean all men are the same, or even that it would happen again.

I know it won't. I won't let it. Now go away.

It's my job to tell you when you're veering off path, and this is a definite detour.

How is helping others and stopping a killer, considered a detour? I thought that's what I was here to do.

You're ignoring the real issue of your heart, and when you start down that road, it's going to be even harder to get back on course. A part of your soul will start to wilt.

It already has, Sophie announced and reopened her eyes in an attempt to shut Will out. She didn't want to think about Jack. She was still trying to wipe the images from her mind. His reason, his excuse, the pleading look he'd given her, none of it mattered if they were all dead. None of it mattered regardless. She pushed the memories away.

Ben held her gaze from across the table. He'd been a silent witness to the betrayal. A hint of pity stared back at her. A simple kind of knowing was exchanged between them, one of those unspoken shared meanings that Sophie used to hate when she noticed the same look between Jack and Marshall. She broke the connection and looked away, pushing back the tears for a more appropriate time. She pulled out the manila file again from her backpack and reread the information for the millionth time, hoping to figure out something she'd missed. Whatever it was, she missed it again. Sophie rubbed her tired eyes and looked around the empty cabin of the company jet. All of the ghosts from the last few days appeared to be along for the ride, though none of them were talking to her. They just stared at her, expecting her to have or find the answers. A feat that she wasn't sure she could tackle.

Sophie pulled in a deep breath and exhaled. Was their presence an omen?

"You all right, Sophie?" Aiden asked.

Sophie felt the blood draining from her face as she shook her head. "They're here."

"Who?" Ben asked as he leaned over the table, looking around the empty plane. "Who's here?"

"All of them." Sophie nodded to the empty seats around the plane. "Ryan, his sister Macy, and Janice. It appears they're along for the ride."

Ben's brows dipped as he glanced around the cabin. "What are they doing?"

She shrugged. "Nothing. Not even talking."

Aiden laid his hand down over hers and gave a gentle squeeze. "Try asking them who killed them. See if they'll tell us and save us a trip."

"I've already tried that." Sophie rolled her eyes. "You do realize they can hear you?"

Aiden's mouth parted. "Well then..." Aiden repeated it louder and much slower, as if talking to a foreigner. "Tell us who killed you."

None of them responded. They each had a sad look in their eyes as they glanced around at the occupants of the cabin before suddenly vanishing out of sight.

"What did they say?" Ben prompted.

"You scared them away." Sophie's lips slid into a smile. "They said to figure it out yourself."

"No, they didn't."

Her grin grew bigger. "No...they didn't. They didn't say anything, just vanished."

"Is that typical ghost behavior?" Aiden asked.

"There's nothing typical about any of them. Not one word." She turned to look at Aiden. "Most have a ton to say. Tell Aunt Mary I left the will in the drawer. Tell Uncle James to spend more time with the kids. But not these three. Not a peep. If I didn't know any better, I would think they were banned from talking to me, period."

That thought set her blood boiling. Was it possible for Will to keep the others from interacting with her, or was she just being paranoid?

"Just breathe, Sophie." Aiden removed his hand. "I'd hate to have to order an emergency landing because you passed out from hyperventilating. I'm sure Marshall would kick my ass."

"Marshall left the office hours before we did." Sophie released a breath she didn't realize she was holding. "Besides, I have a feeling you can take him."

Aiden's look turned to one of faint amusement. "I learned my lesson the hard way, the first time he kicked my ass."

"I'm sure you didn't do anything to deserve that," Sophie added, a bit of humor and sarcasm in her voice.

Ben chuckled. "Of course, he didn't."

****

An hour later they were all situated in a four-bedroom penthouse suite compliments of Dixon Security. They had separate bedrooms and an adjoining common area and kitchen where they were setting up camp. They were all in for the night, planning to get a fresh start in the morning. Sophie dropped her bag by the bed and fell backward onto the plush comforter, her eyes on the ceiling, her mind and heart elsewhere. She heard the familiar beep of a new text message and pulled her phone out of her pocket.

Marshall. *I'm glad you made it.*

Sophie smiled and began to type. *Everything is quiet on our end. We haven't started to stir the natives yet. They don't even know we're here.*

"Don't be so sure. I've already gotten a call."

Sophie sat up right on the bed, her fingers flying over the keyboard. *"Who and how?"*

"Airport police. Tiny town and airport. Everyone knows everyone, especially since the flight plan included my company's name. By morning, everyone will know who you are."

"So much for the element of surprise."

"Do you like surprises?" he asked.

She didn't reply.

"Be careful and stick to Aiden like glue. You aren't in this alone."

"10-4," Sophie answered and tossed her phone onto the bedside table. Another beep had her reaching for it.

This time it wasn't Marshall who texted her; it was Jack. *"We need to talk when you get back."*

"No, we don't."

"There are some things you need to know."

"Unless it's about Covington and the killer, there's nothing we need to say."

"Sophie, baby."

"Is that what you called her too?" She typed the last words with anger and hurt.

There was a long pause while Sophie clutched the phone to her chest, and a tear slid down her cheek and into her hair. Now wasn't the time for a breakdown. She could do that when the killer was behind bars.

Knuckles wrapped on her door, pulling her from her thoughts. She slid off the bed and padded over to the door. "Who is it?"

"Housekeeping," Aiden answered in a high-pitched voice, doing his best impression of a woman. She grinned. "I came to fluff your pillow."

She chuckled as she pulled the door open.

He tossed her a pair of boxers and a long T-shirt. "Go change."

She held up the clothes and tilted her head. "I'm not ready for bed." She tossed them back.

His grin grew bigger. "That's good." He tossed them back. "Those aren't for bed. Besides I was hoping you slept in the nude."

"Not that you'll ever know." She walked into the bathroom and started to strip. "Tell me again why I'm changing into your clothes. Is this your idea of undercover because, if it is, you suck at the element of surprise."

She pulled the door open. His shirt hung down to her knees.

"Don't you look cute," he joked.

She planted her hand on her hip, and he grabbed it and pulled her out into the living room. He grabbed three beers from the fridge and led her out of the suite, steering her out onto the exit stairwell.

"Where are we going?" she demanded, taking two steps for every one of his.

"To have some fun."

He twisted off the top of her beer and handed her one, leaving him still carrying two. Sophie ignored her apprehension of running around an unfamiliar hotel in just boxers and a T-shirt and followed next to Aiden. He pulled the stairwell exit door open and guided her down another long hallway before emerging into an atrium.

She stopped just inside the door. Large potted plants surrounded the room, creating a feeling of privacy. Concrete and brick pavers covered the floor that led to a pool. Tables and chairs surrounded the area. It wasn't the pool that made her pause. Most hotels had them. It was the hunky, shirtless man standing in swim trunks at the edge of the pool. A smile stretched across his lips, provoking one of her own. The tension in her shoulders began to fade. No matter whether she was mad at him or happy with him, his presence alone offered her a strength she didn't know she had.

The little shit had shown up and texted her like he was a million miles away.

"Wipe that smirk off your face," she announced while taking a swig of her beer before setting it down on the nearest table.

"Why? What are you going to do if I don't?" Marshall asked.

She grinned as she approached him. Not thinking before she acted, she pushed him backward. His hand snaked around her waist, and she was dragged into the water with him. They both emerged laughing and sputtering water, and then she swam to the shallow end to regain her footing.

Marshall wiped the water from his face, a grin still on his lips. "I've fired people for less."

"He has," Aiden agreed before doing a cannonball, landing next to Marshall and soaking him again.

She sprawled out on her back, letting the buoyancy of the water keep her a float. "We both know you're too stubborn to fire me. It would mean you were wrong."

Marshall wiped the splash from his face and grinned. "Maybe not you, but him....That's a good possibility."

Aiden stood, the top of his chest poking out of the water. "You won't fire me either. I brought the girl and the beer."

Marshall shrugged. "You have a good point."

Aiden dunked Sophie under water, making her sputter as she rose from the water. She slicked her hair back out of her face. "What are you doing here? Didn't you trust us to get the job done?"

"I figured it couldn't hurt to have an extra pair of eyes and ears. Are you surprised?"

Her lips tilted up in a half smirk. "Not really."

Sophie sunk beneath the water and re-emerged a few feet away from him. "I need a favor."

Marshall grinned. "You need me to tuck you in."

"That's my job," Aiden complained.

"That's not what I'm talking about." She righted the rising T-shirt ballooned by the water, pulling it back down to cover her stomach. "I need Ben, or whoever pulled the bank records when we needed them on my cold case. Do you think they can do it again?"

"Sure, who do you need it on?"

"Everyone that just died and the people left that know your secret."

"Consider it done."

Sophie snuggled in the complimentary towel to block the coolness of the air conditioning on her way back up to the room. She'd needed that little break. The swim had done her mood and head wonders. It was refreshing and fun, and she couldn't remember the last time she'd enjoyed herself to that extent. Her tired, fatigued muscles fought as she entered her freezing room. She hurried to the air conditioner and adjusted the settings before hopping in the shower to enjoy the welcoming warm water. She changed into a tank top and her yoga pants before she crawled into the bed. She scheduled a wake-up call for six in the morning and, unable to keep her eyes open, promptly fell asleep to the low sound of the television.

She drifted in a restless sleep that included a guided tour, like a replay, of all of the deaths that surrounded her. The four women from the cold case and now Ryan, Macy, and Janice were added to the list. She hadn't been privy to the killings, but their ghosts and all of the places and words they'd ever exchanged entered her mind. It was as though her dreams were terrorizing her, taunting her, making her question why she'd chosen her path, instead of being the encouragement she needed to continue.

Sophie's eyes popped open to the sound of the phone ringing next to the bed. She reached for it and mumbled a thank you to the employee that had woken her. She plopped back down on the pillow and wiped the sleep from her tired eyes. Today, she was one step closer to finding the killer, one step closer to bringing a bit of justice to Ryan's family and Jack and Marshall's ex-girlfriend.

Knuckles rapped on her door, making her drag herself out of bed. She yanked the door open before even asking who was on the other side, her tired mind still not functioning to perfection.

Marshall was fully dressed and smiling at her. He had Styrofoam coffee cups in a carrier in one hand and a bakery bag in his other.

"Tell me you brought me chocolate."

He winked. "I did."

"Good man." She held the door open for him and followed him back into the room. She grabbed one of the coffees before sliding the bag from his hand and plopping back down on the bed. "Why are you up so early?"

"Why are you?"

She shook her head while peering into the bag and coming up with a chocolate-covered donut from the top of the pile. "You can't answer my question with a question."

Marshall kicked his shoes off and climbed up on the bed with her. He grabbed his own donut before leaning against the headboard and crossing his feet at the ankles. "I didn't sleep well. Being back in this town has me on edge."

"Football hero returning home. Were you expecting a parade or a harem of women waiting?"

Marshall chuckled before sipping his coffee. "Hardly, that would have been Jack. He was the hero jock. I was just his sidekick, who happened to be good at sports."

She swallowed her bite and licked her fingers as she moved to lean against the headboard next to him. "I doubt that. I'm sure you were both adored." Her lips tilted up in a grin. "So do I get to meet your parents today? Any psychotic sisters I need to know about?"

"You've met my family already."

Sophie's smile slipped. Her only memory of meeting any of his relatives involved meetings of the spirit kind. A grandmother, a grandfather, and his sister. No parents or other siblings had appeared to wish him a happy birthday.

"I've met your grandparents and sister. Surely you have a mom and dad too."

"Doesn't everyone?" he whispered and let his head fall back against the wall. "Mine weren't the kind you see on TV. They were irresponsible drunks and drug addicts that didn't have the time to raise two kids."

"I'm sorry." She laid her hand over his and gave a gentle squeeze.

He rested his on top of hers and turned to look into her eyes. "Don't be sorry for me. My grandparents were great people. We might not have been rich, but what we lacked in money, we received in their devotion and love. No amount of money in the world can buy that."

His grandparents probably made him into the man he was today. Brilliant, honest, and devoted. The SEALs probably had a bit of influence over his morals, but if she had to guess, it was his grandparents doing. That and the accident probably molded him into the man sitting next to her today.

She slid off the bed and started rummaging through her suitcase, pulling out clothes and her cosmetic bag. "Okay, I'm going to go get ready, so why don't you think about where we need to start?"

"This is your show. Where do you suggest?"

Sophie held the clothes against her chest. His reply caught her off guard. Was this a test? Did he really trust that she could figure this out?

"I suggest we start with the obvious."

He arched his brow. "Who do you consider obvious?"

"The coach, the cop, Ryan's family, and Janice's," she said, ticking them off with her fingers. "After that we'll create a web around them and work our way out."

"What are we looking for?"

She shrugged. "Alibis for the last week, money transactions, and motive - no matter how petty. We check it all."

Sophie headed toward the bathroom.

"I knew I was right about you." Marshall's lips quirked as he fought back the smile twisting his lips. Sophie paused at his words, turning to lean against the doorframe.

"Gifted, beautiful, and smart." He held her gaze.

"I guess that makes you brilliant for hiring me," she quipped.

He smiled. "Did you doubt me?"

"It was touch and go when we first met."

She smirked before disappearing into the bathroom, where she started getting ready for the long day ahead of her.

****

Sophie took her time in the bathroom, and Marshall didn't move. The television was on, the volume low. She'd either been watching it last night or this morning. The weather skirted across the screen. The hurricane that was headed their way was due to arrive at the end of the week. If they were lucky, they'd be long gone before it hit. Sophie's phone vibrated next to the bed.

"Sophie, someone is calling you."

"Answer it," she hollered through the door.

Marshall picked up her phone and hit the answer button. "Masterson's phone."

"Where is Masterson, and who is this?" Amber asked.

"This is Marshall, and Sophie's in the shower. Who is this?"

"Her best friend. What are you doing answering her phone? Though a better question is, what are you doing in her room if you aren't in the shower with her?"

"Ha." He laughed. "Amber, I like the way you think. Unfortunately for me, she didn't invite me to take one with her."

"Since when do you need an invitation?"

"Good point." Had he screwed up by not going after her like he did everything else in his life? Had he turned complacent because he didn't want to hurt his best friend? The way he was treating Sophie was inconsistent with the approach he used for everything else. Maybe he needed to kiss her again, remind her what she was missing. Would he be able to stop at just one?

"Ah....silence. Does that mean you're thinking about hanging up on me and barging in on her?"

"Nothing so bold, not yet."

"So, care to clue me in on your intentions for my best friend?"

His lips tilted up in a grin as he countered. "Care to clue me in on yours for Beau?"

"Jury is still out," she answered.

"Where is he by the way? Did you kick him out?"

"He's sleeping, and as for kicking him out, I don't see that happening. He's leaving me too exhausted to think straight."

"Then why are you calling? Did you need to speak with her?"

"No, actually I needed to talk to you. The media got news about the murders."

"How the hell did that happen?"

"Not sure, but they know details. They keep flashing pictures of Jack and Janice in a restaurant together. They even have one of Jack and Sophie in her house."

"Shit."

They're hinting at a triangle between Sophie, Jack, and Janice. They're portraying Jack as a cheater and Sophie a relationship wrecker. The way they're making it sound is that Janice was murdered to get her out of the picture."

Marshall slid his legs off the bed and squeezed his eyes closed. "How the hell did they get pictures?"

"I don't know. I called Sophie's sister-in-law to find out what's going on, and she told me Max mentioned DNA under the woman's nails....Jack's DNA, and on top of that, there's a money transfer that they aren't making public yet. Max is working like a maniac to figure out what the hell is going on, and he's taking a hit too. He is her brother."

Marshall clenched his eyes closed and let his head fall forward. He heard the shower stop, and dread filled his stomach. How was he going to explain this to Sophie? "Tell Beau I'll be in touch and to call and tell Dash and Roman, along with their teams, to come back from their missions. We're going after this bastard with all that we've got."

"Okay."

Marshall slid the phone off in time to hear the hair dryer going. He pulled out his own cell phone, fired off a text to the pilot to remain on standby, one to Ben to start the trace into finding the media's informant, and last but not least, one to his attorney to start actions of a lawsuit against the media and to be prepared for all of the backlash.

He rapped on the door. She didn't answer over the sound of the hair dryer, so he turned the knob and opened the door, hoping she wouldn't get too mad over his intrusion.

She stood in her bra and matching panties and met his gaze in the mirror. Her body and face were flushed from the heated room. His mind went blank as he stared at her perfection. He hardened as she licked her lips. She held the hair dryer over her head with one hand, and the wind blew her long strands straight as she used the brush to comb them into place. She clicked it off and turned to face him, not embarrassed and unashamed that she was standing in front of him almost naked. It wouldn't take him but a few seconds to have her stripped the rest of the way and then be savoring every inch of her body.

"What?" she asked as she turned to face him, setting the dryer and brush down. "What happened?"

"You're beautiful," Marshall whispered before clearing his throat. His gaze travelled back up her body.

Her face flushed even darker as she grabbed the nearby towel and wrapped it around her body.

He stepped into the bathroom. Unhooking her towel, he dropped it and let it pool around her feet. He pushed the stuff on the counter back and lifted her to sit on it, moving to stand between her legs. His body pressed to her most private part, his lips mere inches from hers.

"What are you doing?" she asked breathlessly.

"Savoring you," he whispered into her ear, his lips a breath away from her creamy skin. It took every bit of willpower not to break her trust, not to pursue her further. His fingers trailed a path down her arms before he held her at the waist.

"You promised."

He leaned his forehead against hers and closed his eyes. "I know." He opened his eyes and held her gaze. "This is me promising. I haven't kissed you. You're still wearing your bra and panties, and no matter how badly I ache to touch you, to taste you, to be inside you"—he inhaled a deep breath and exhaled—"I haven't. Not yet."

"Marshall..."

He cleared his throat and stepped back, away from the warmth of her body. "We have a problem."

"What?" She hopped down off the counter and followed him out of the bathroom.

He kept his back to her, and his head drooped forward. "I don't know how to tell you this."

She touched his arm, turning him around. "Just tell me."

He held her gaze while repeating everything he'd just been told.

Her mouth parted in sheer shock as she plopped down on the bed.

He sat down next to her and reached for her hand, squeezing it in his, her near-nakedness making it hard for him to stay focused. "They're trying to pin this on Jack."

"I have to go." She held his gaze, and beneath her bra, her chest heaved. She stood and started scanning the room for her things.

"What are you going to do, Sophie? Don't give them any more ammunition. The best way we can help Jack is to figure out who the hell is behind this."

She whirled around on Marshall, ripples of shock riddling her face. "We can't let him deal with this alone. He would never abandon us."

Marshall stood and walked over to her, placing his palms on her arms, her bare skin soft beneath his touch. "We aren't abandoning him. I've called in all the teams, my attorney, and every resource I have to help him and you. We're hitting this head-on. No running, no hiding." His lips quirked. "We both know you never would."

His eye searched hers while he watched her facial features change from determination to eventually softening into understanding. "We find the source, smash it like a bug, and get this bastard and throw his ass in jail."

A burning fire flickered in her determined eyes. "Why don't you call Jack to check in while I get dressed? The quicker we work, the faster we'll get back."

9 CHAPTER

Sophie and Marshall met Aiden and Ben outside the hotel lobby. Ben was behind the wheel of a dark, four-door SUV, and Aiden was leaning against the passenger door. He had his arms crossed over his chest, and he appeared to be relaxed while he waited. Dark shades covered his blue eyes. He'd opted for jeans and a T-shirt as if to fit in like a native, yet his overpowering presence had him sticking out like a sore thumb. In a small town of locals, any hot outsiders with big muscles were going to get noticed and admired. He pushed off from the door and moved to open the back door for them to climb in.

"Good morning," Sophie said while walking up to him.

"I'm sorry about Jack," Aiden announced as he placed his palm on her arm. "You know that we won't let anything happen to him."

"I know." Her words came out a whisper as she patted his hand. "Let's find this asshole so we can go home."

She slid into the back seat followed by Marshall, who pulled the door closed. Her gaze met Ben's in the rearview mirror. His eyes were puffy as he sipped coffee.

"You didn't sleep well either?" she asked him.

He shook his head. "I was up all night pulling financial records."

Sophie's eyes widened as she leaned forward, waiting for Aiden to click his seatbelt. "Anything interesting?"

Ben's features clouded before he quickly masked the look and answered, "Not yet." He cleared his throat. "Where are we going first?"

"How about we start with the easiest first and work our way out? Let's start with your coach."

"Great idea," Marshall agreed.

Ben pulled out of the parking lot and drove them through town. Sophie's gaze stared out the window, even with her mind elsewhere. The town was small. They stopped at a red light next to a grocery store and Sophie watched as people scurried in and out. Men stood on ladders with drills in hand outside the grocery store, securing plywood into place to cover the plate glass windows. Bottles of water and groceries were being lugged into the back of SUV's, trucks, and cars.

"If the hurricane isn't supposed to hit for another week, why is everyone getting prepared now? Did something change?" Sophie asked, turning her gaze to the front of the car.

"I saw on the local news last night that the hurricane has picked up speed and is getting bigger. They're expecting a category four, so we need to be long gone before it hits," Ben answered.

"How long do we have?"

"We'll start to feel the outer bands in about another day, so my guess is we have about two days to get the hell out of dodge before they ground all flights," Marshall answered.

"That's not much time." Sophie replied, sinking back into her seat. She rubbed at her temples, trying to stave off the forming headache from the imposed time crunch.

They pulled up along the curb outside of a small brick home. The lawn was green, just a little overgrown. The shrubs had seen better days. Little lawn gnomes were out on display around the trees, some knocked over and lying in the dirt. An older woman with white hair poking out from under her wide brim hat rested on her knees, pulling out weeds in a small garden of flowers. An oversized, older car was parked in the driveway. Sheets of plywood rested against the house under the carport.

She stood and turned toward the car while wiping her hands on her dirty apron.

They all got out, Ben and Marshall leading the way.

"Mrs. Gertie," Marshall announced, holding out his arms in welcome to the older woman before pulling her in for a hug. The woman's smile was genuine and warm. Affection glistened in her eyes as she smiled back.

"Marshall Dixon, it's been a long time." She grinned before turning to Ben. "And Ben Adams. What on earth are you doing back in town?"

"We just came into town to see the coach. Is he around?" Ben grinned and looked expectantly toward the house.

Gertie's lips slipped from a smile into a frown, her face looking more tired than just moments ago, as if the happiness was just sucked out of her. She masked it just as quickly. She swiped the beaded sweat from her brow. "It sure is hot out here. Why don't you and your friends come inside? I'll pour us some tea, and I'll tell you all about it."

She headed back into the house, not waiting to see if Marshall, Ben, Aiden, and Sophie would follow, yet they did. The house was dark, even with the shades drawn open. There was a depressed feeling in the air. The dainty flowered doilies matched the furniture. Sophie glanced at a picture of Gertie and an older man while the woman set a pitcher of tea on the table and started filling glasses and handing them out.

"Who are your friends?" she asked Marshall and Ben while smiling warming at Aiden and Sophie.

Marshall leaned back against the couch and rested his ankle on his opposite knee. "Coworkers that I wanted to introduce to Coach. Is he around?"

An apparition appeared behind Gertie's chair, his hand on her shoulder. He was the man in the pictures on display in the living room. He looked down at his wife before lifting his head and holding Sophie's gaze. Her eyes narrowed in disbelief. He moved away from his wife and Sophie followed his movement. He tilted his head and she tilted hers, mimicking him to let him know she could see him.

"We're too late," Sophie whispered beneath her breath. Marshall and Aiden gave her a confused look.

Gertie looked down into her cup of tea. Her shoulders deflated. "Sorry, Marshall, you missed him by two weeks."

"Oh?" Ben replied, turning to face Gertie again.

"He died two weeks ago from a massive heart attack."

The room became silent. The heaviness in the air was smothering. Marshall slid off the couch and crouched in front of Gertie, and his hands clasped hers. "I'm so sorry. I didn't know..."

She patted his hand. "He had a good life. He loved you boys, his job and me. I'm sure he's happy and looking down on all of us."

The ghost across the room rolled his eyes, making Sophie's mouth part in surprise. She cleared her throat.

"Excuse me. Do you have a restroom I can use?"

Ben looked at Sophie like she'd grown a second head, and Aiden just watched her with curiosity.

"Sure, dear, it's down that hall, the second door on the right."

"Thank you," Sophie answered as she rose. She held the spirit's gaze and motioned with her head down the hall as if to get him to follow. She kept walking without looking back or knowing if he would follow. She hoped he would but wouldn't be surprised if the man didn't trust her intentions. Hell, she didn't trust her intentions.

Sophie glanced behind her as she entered the small bathroom; the hall was empty. She walked in and closed the door. The spirit of the coach floated in front of her. "Why are you in my house?"

This was a first for Sophie. A hostile ghost that didn't want or need her help. Or so the Coach thought.

"You do know you're dead, right?"

"Are you slow, woman? She just told you I was dead."

Sophie shrugged. "Just making sure." She moved farther into the bathroom and glanced out the window.

"What do you want!" the coach bellowed.

"I want answers. Within the last couple of days, two members from your community have been killed and they both knew my friends, Jack Love and Marshall Dixon. I need to know if there is anyone you can think of who didn't like either of them."

The ghost watched her every movement. "I don't know you. And why would I tell you anything to help those boys? After everything I did for them. What did they ever do for me? I'll tell you what they did. They managed to ruin my career. We never won another game once those two gave up the sport. They abandoned not only me, but the other people who counted on them."

"Why didn't your nephew, Mark, step in to play?"

The Coach pressed his lips together refusing to answer.

"Fine, don't answer me. I'll figure it out. I thought you ghosts were supposed to be all love and light."

"Ha." He shook his head. "You don't know me."

"Obviously." Why would the coach help her if he didn't have anything to gain? "They were just kids."

"They were my ticket out of this town into a better coaching position. Instead, I was stuck with kids like that little twerp Ben out there who didn't know a football from a baseball."

Sophie's brow cocked, her arms folded against her chest. "I don't think you know anything. You're just a bitter old spirit. Is that why you haven't gone into the white light? You aren't ready to let go? You have unfinished business here?"

The ghost was standing by the sink one minute and the next by the door. "Leave, now!"

Sophie reached through his body and turned the handle on the door. She pulled it open and paused. "Oh, before I leave, I have one question for you."

The apparition looked agitated that she hadn't left.

"Do you watch the news?"

He didn't answer. There was no smart remark, no venom of hate spewed at her. She held in her triumphant smile. She had him right where she wanted him, and they both knew it.

"Yeah…I guess I'll just take those big beefy guys with me when I leave. It's a shame really. I'm sure they could have hung those boards up on her windows in less than fifteen minutes." Sophie shrugged.

"You'd use my wife to blackmail me! You're no better than they are." The ghost's voice boomed, filling the air around her and giving her a headache.

Sophie eased the door shut one more time. "Listen here, old man." She sneered. "Those are my friends, and I will help them by any means necessary. So don't you lecture me about morals, you asshole. You're the one who broke the law;

you're the one who covered up the accident, and you're the one who's going to help me because you love your wife. Now, if you don't want me to leave without helping her, I suggest you start talking."

He remained quiet, even while shooting daggers with his gaze.

Sophie shrugged. "Fine, have it your way."

"You wouldn't."

She grinned. "I would."

"I don't have much to tell."

"Start talking."

A knock interrupted their conversation.

"Sophie, are you okay?" Marshall whispered from the other side of the door.

"Yeah, just tell her I don't feel well." She eased the door open so he could see her face. "I need you to stall. I need you guys to go put up the plywood to cover her windows and secure anything else you see that might get damaged by the storm."

His look was puzzled, but he didn't question her directives. He just nodded and left her in the bathroom.

"Who are you?" the ghost asked.

"Who I am doesn't matter."

He regarded her in silence before he started talking. "Those boys were town favorites."

"That's not what I want to know. Let's start with who had access to the vodka. Do you have any idea who actually spiked it, or who could have spiked it?"

"No one knows who did it, not even the police. Ryan threw a house party. The entire student body was suspect."

"Well, that's not very helpful. Who else knew about the accident?"

The ghost moved to the window and looked out. "My brother, the families, and whoever they told." He turned back to Sophie. "This is a small town. Word travels fast."

"What do you know about Janice Miller?"

That question caught the Coach off guard. She saw confusion written on his ghostly features. "She was easy. She liked my athletes, and for some reason, they liked her. She was the reason for several fights in school, out of school, and just in general, but if you ask me, that girl was manipulative. She used her body to get what she wanted, and most of the time she got whatever she set her eye on."

"Even Mark?"

The ghost outright laughed in her face. "No, not Mark."

"Why not him?"

Coach grinned. "He batted for the other team."

Sophie hadn't been expecting that answer. With guys like Jack and Marshall, who could have wanted or needed more?

"Sweetie, are you all right?" Gertie asked from the other side of the door. "Can I get you some water or anything?"

Sophie turned on the faucet and splashed water on her face. She used the towel hanging from the spindle to dab at her skin. "I'll be back if I need more answers," she whispered to the ghost before pulling the door open and coming face to face with the ghost's wife.

"I'm sorry. I'm not feeling so hot."

Gertie took Sophie's arm and led her back down the hall. "Would you like to rest in the spare room?"

"Oh no, I couldn't impose. I'm going to go check on the guys to see I can help so we can get out of your hair."

Sophie took the woman's hands in hers. "I'm sorry for your loss." Sophie pulled a card out of her purse and handed it to Gertie. "I know we just met, but if you ever need anything, please call me. I know how important the Coach was to my friends, and that practically makes you family."

The coach had appeared behind his wife and was listening to the exchange.

"You would have helped her anyway," he stated as if knowing her reply.

Sophie couldn't hide her grin; she winked in his direction before she left them both standing in the living room. This new bit of information put a damper on her investigation. She knew Janice had been loose, but between that and the spiked alcohol, it could have been anyone they were associated with.

Sophie stepped out into the late afternoon heat. Wind blew her hair in her face as she followed the path that lead to the back of the house. The guys had two more windows to do and glanced her way as she neared.

"You feeling okay?" Aiden asked, a little too loudly, in case someone was listening.

"I'll be fine. Are you guys almost done?"

Aiden grinned as he stepped down from the ladder and reached for the last sheet of plywood to secure in place.

Ben pulled out the keys and tossed them to her. "Why don't you go sit in the car while we finish up?"

She placed a small smile on her face and left them to finish with the plywood and whatever else they needed to do.

Sophie slid behind the steering wheel, started the car, and then turned on the air conditioner. The hot humid air was stifling, almost suffocating. The calm before the storm?

Sophie pulled her phone out of her purse and punched in Jack's number. She was planning on leaving a message when he actually answered. "Soph."

"Hi, Jack. Are you all right?"

"I'll be better when we catch this guy." Jack sounded stressed.

"I'm working on it." She took a deep breath. "Listen...I just called because I thought you should know. Your Coach died two weeks ago from a heart attack. I'm sorry."

Silence briefly filled the line before he replied again. "When are you coming back?"

Sophie bit her bottom lip. She didn't have the answer to that. "I'm not sure. Hopefully, before the hurricane hits, but it may be longer. Marshall told me about what they're splashing on the news. How are you holding up?"

"I'll survive." He cleared his throat. "Listen, I'm sorry you're involved in this. I've made mistakes and now your name is being smeared along with mine. I never meant for my past to touch you."

"Well then, I guess we need to set the record straight and get this all sorted out." She paused, not sure if she wanted to know the answer to her next question. "How come you didn't tell me about the restaurant?"

"Sophie..." His words trailed off as she bit back the sting in her eyes and the tightening around her heart.

"Never mind. I don't want to know," she decided. "One of us will call you with updates. Keep us posted on what's going on."

The line went silent again as she waited for his response. "We had dinner once. Nothing happened, Sophie. Nothing but the kiss you already saw."

"Jack." She lifted her head and opened her eyes to find Marshall, Aiden, and Ben walking to the car. "I have to go."

"Sophie, wait… Tell me you believe me."

Slowly she shook her head. "I…have to go."

She hung up the phone just as the others slid into the car. Aiden turned in his seat. His gaze assessing as she tried to hide evidence of her hurt heart.

Ben glanced backward. "Where to?"

"Breakfast, so we can make a game plan."

Aiden turned around as Ben started to drive. Marshall's gaze held hers. He didn't ask any questions, just reached for her hand and laced their fingers together in the silent support she needed.

Aiden was the first to break the silence. "So what was the delay for back there?"

"The coach was hanging around, and let me tell you, he's a grouchy old geezer. He wasn't going to tell me anything until I told him we wouldn't help Gertie until he did."

Ben's gaze met hers in the rearview mirror. "What did he say?"

She shrugged, unsure how much to tell Ben. She didn't want to hurt his feelings. She didn't want to ruin any fond memories he or the others had of the old bastard. "He said that Janice slept around."

"We already knew that," Ben answered.

"He also suggested that Ryan had a party at his house and anyone could have tampered with the vodka."

"So, it's going to be like looking for a needle in a haystack," Marshall replied.

"I'm afraid so." Sophie mulled around the information in her head. The visit had produced more questions than answers. Someone who attended the party and knew Jack, Marshall, and Janice was the probable killer. Did Mark factor into any of this? He hadn't even played the next year, but his quick departure out of town left her with more questions. It was just going to be a matter of narrowing down the list. "Do you think we can get a yearbook or a list of students?"

"Sure. That shouldn't be too hard. All I have to do is hack the school's database and see if they still have the information from back then."

"Perfect," she answered.

****

After eating breakfast, they dropped Ben off at the hotel so he could get started on obtaining the list she needed and get back to work on the financials she'd asked for. Aiden stayed behind also to do some online research in the attempt to figure out who was behind the media leak and to see if they'd made any progress on the video feed in her apartment.

"Where too?" Marshall asked as he shifted the SUV gear into drive.

"Let's start with Chief Campbell. I'd really like to know why he sent Mark away after the accident."

"Do you think he's going to talk?"

149

She shrugged. "It's worth a try."

The entire drive to the police station, Sophie replayed everything over in her head that she knew; the guys, Janice, Macy, and Mark. She was missing something, she just didn't know what.

Marshall parked out front and they entered the building. Sophie had been expecting a few cops sitting around drinking coffee in the small town, yet the room was a buzz. The phones were ringing off the hook as cops scurried around. Marshall leaned into her side and whispered. "Early hurricane preparations."

She gave a slow nod as she walked up to the desk and asked to speak with the Captain.

They were told he was in a meeting with the Emergency Operations Center Team and would be busy all day.

Sophie shoulders deflated. She was hoping to get a reason for Mark's departure but it looked like that answer was going to have to wait.

Sophie and Marshall left and got back in the SUV.

"We'll have to try later. Where to next?"

"We need to go see Ryan's family." She turned in her seat. "This may be a bit hard for you."

Marshall pressed his lips together and started driving. "I guess there's no time like the present." He glanced at her. "It may not be a very warm welcome if they know Macy died."

"Losing one kid in a lifetime would be hard enough for any parent. I can't imagine what their mom is going through with losing two."

Sophie let the silence in the SUV engulf her while she sat lost in her own thoughts. She was failing Jack. They'd come searching for answers and had discovered more questions than anything else. The killer could be anyone with a grudge. Her confidence was slowly dissipating, even as her determination strengthened. Marshall slowed as they passed a painted cross sitting upright on the side of the road. The cross was old and tattered. It looked worn over time from the elements, but Ryan's name was written in black across the front. Flowers surrounded the spot where Sophie assumed the accident had taken place. She reached for Marshall's hand and linked their fingers, giving a gentle squeeze, the same kind of support he'd shown her in the car. It was no wonder they'd all moved, no longer wanting to live with the memories surrounding their best friend's death.

Farther up the road, groves of peach trees lined the fields until the road opened up onto flat land. Marshall turned down a long drive that led to a two-story white house with blue shutters. Three cars were parked in the circular drive in front of the house. The yard was perfectly landscaped. Candles were lit in the upstairs windows, as if to light the way home.

Marshall parked the car and got out, meeting her at the front of the SUV. She looked up at the windows again where the lights flickered. "Are you sure they know?"

The screen door flew open, banging against the house as a man a little older than her and Marshall came flying out and down the steps. He converged on Marshall, shoving him against the SUV. "How dare you show up here?"

The dark-haired man threw the first punch. There was a split second when Marshall could have blocked it, could have stopped the punishing hit from landing, yet he didn't.

Marshall's head jerked to the side from the impact and Sophie pushed between the two, blocking the asshole from striking again.

"Move or I'll hit you too."

"I'd like to see you try," Sophie dared, balling her fist by her side.

"Sophie, don't..." Marshall tried to pull her back behind him. She jerked her arm out of his grasp and stood her ground. The man was big, and she may have been an idiot for egging the asshole on, but she wasn't Marshall. She'd go down with a fight.

"You asked for it." His gaze narrowed, and she lifted her fist, ready to try and take the jerk on.

"Cord Michael." A woman's voice pierced the air, the yell coming from the porch. "What the hell is wrong with you!"

The woman scurried down the steps and stepped between Sophie and the jerk. "In the house, now!"

The guy didn't make any attempt to move. The woman planted her hands on her hips and shoved his arm toward the house. "I said move it, buster."

"But, Mom, they're dead because of him."

"No, baby." Her voice softened. "They're dead because they both made bad choices. Ryan was drinking and driving. Marshall could be in the grave next to him, and then how would you feel, knowing your brother took innocent lives with him? Marshall didn't kill them. He may have been there, but he didn't drive the car, and he didn't shoot your sister."

She planted her palm on his arm. "They just messed up, baby." A tear escaped the woman's eyes and rolled down her face. "They just messed up, Cord."

Cord's face remained red and blotchy. He stared at Sophie and Marshall with daggers of hate. This guy, Cord, was placing blame where it didn't necessarily belong, and even with his mother's words, Sophie didn't think he was ready to back down. The tension in the air got thicker with every second the guy remained standing there. Mrs. Reyes continued, trying to break through to her son so he could reach a point of comprehension and understanding. Sophie squeezed her purse, recognizing the lumpy hard feel of the weapon inside. Just one wrong move, one threat, and she'd shoot him in the knee, something to slow the asshole down and stop him from hurting either of them again. She was unwilling to take away the remaining child from this family.

Sophie's gaze remained locked on his. She projected no hesitation and no fear back at the jerk, a move that her brother had taught her long ago. He'd said, "When dealing with bullies, you don't back down. You stand up straight and wait for the punches to land and hope to get in a couple of your own." Only she wasn't that little awkward girl anymore, the one that needed saving. She could handle this emotionally distraught guy. She *would* handle this emotionally distraught guy if his mother couldn't.

"We didn't come here looking for trouble. We came to pay our respects and ask you some questions. We're here to hunt down Ryan and Macy's killers. Now you can either respect that, and help us, or not. The call is yours, but let me make one thing very clear, Cord. Jack and Marshall are like family to me. They might not be blood like Ryan and Macy are to you, but they are *my* family, and you won't touch Marshall again or threaten me." Sophie ignored the gasp from Cord's mother and stepped up next to her. "It's your call. Are you going to help, or do you want us to leave? Once we leave, it's over. We'll give up on our pursuit to bring their killers to justice."

Ryan appeared right next to his brother, his gaze going back and forth between Sophie and Cord. Sophie tried to ignore his presence, not thinking he'd be of any use in this situation.

Tell him he owes me 7.50 and a frog.
I am not telling him that.
Just tell him.

Sophie let out a lengthy breath. "I don't expect you to believe me, but I'm clairvoyant, and your brother is standing next to you."

Cord glanced to his side before meeting her gaze. He didn't seem shocked. He remained silent.

Sophie watched Cord's shoulders ease, any fight leaving with her words.

"He said to tell you that you owe him 7.50 and a frog."

Sophie heard the woman's gasp next to her and turned, reaching for her as the woman's eyes rolled back in her head. Sophie held the woman in her arms and eased both of them down to the ground.

"Mom," Cord shouted and dropped to his knees next to Sophie. He pulled the woman out of Sophie's arms and lifted his mom against his chest. "Come on in."

They followed behind Cord. Marshall gave her a quizzical look, and all Sophie could do was shrug. She had an idea of what was going on, but until she got to talk to Cord, she wasn't sure if what she was picking up on was real or if she was just imagining it.

"Cord, I have to ask—" she said as Marshall held the door open and Cord deposited his mother on the couch, covering her with a blanket.

"Not here," Cord said, cutting her off. He held Marshall's gaze. "Will you watch my mom?"

Marshall nodded and Cord took Sophie by the elbow.

Marshall started to protest. "Sophie…"

She slid her arm out of Cord's grasp.

"I'll be fine," she announced to Marshall and kissed his cheek before walking outside onto the porch and down the steps.

She stopped in the driveway and crossed her arms over her chest as she turned to Cord. "You knew Ryan was there?"

Cord ran his hand through his hair but didn't answer. He didn't have to. She could see the answer on his face.

"Who are you?" Cord asked.

"My name is Sophie Masterson. I work with Marshall in his psychic division and I used to date Jack. They both mean a lot to me."

"Why are you here?"

"We're looking for answers. Someone, with knowledge of your brother, is out to destroy Marshall and Jack, and I'm going to stop them."

"How do Ryan and Macy fit in?"

"I met Macy a few days ago. She was a pawn for whoever was trying to take down Jack and Marshall. She indicated that she knew, and if she didn't play along, then he was going to kill her too."

"Who was going to kill her?"

Sophie shrugged. "She was too scared to tell me before she ran off. I didn't have any idea who

Macy was when we met, much less how she knew Jack and Marshall." Sophie's voice softened. "I'm sorry for your loss."

"And my brother?" Cord asked, his steely gaze holding hers. "How did you meet my brother?"

"I met him afterwards. He told me that Jack and Marshall would be next if I didn't stop the killer."

"You talked to my brother?"

Sophie dropped her arms to her side. "Yes." She tilted her head. "You can't?"

"I can sense him when he's around. I can even see him sometimes, but I normally can't hear him. I can hear others just fine, but for some reason, I have issues hearing him."

"Interesting."

"Why do you say that? Is that not normal?"

She shrugged. "My personal opinion is that the powers-that-be like to censor some spirits. My spirit guide tells me that it's for my own good. Right now, most of them seem to be banned from talking to me. It's supposedly my destiny or path to figure this out without their input. I'm surprised your brother showed up at all, much less spoke to me again. I've been trying to reach him for days without success. I've gotten only a couple flashes of his face after our initial meeting."

"And my sister? Have you seen her spirit too?"

Sophie nodded, her gaze going to her feet. "Right after she was killed. She told me it wasn't my fault. That the killing didn't have anything to do with me. That it was directed toward Jack and Marshall."

She lifted her gaze to meet his. "I tried asking her who killed her, but she vanished. The next time I saw them both was on the plane headed to town. They wouldn't talk to me."

Cord's face softened. "I'm not surprised. He always did defy authority, but he hates it when I fight." Cord cleared his throat. "I'm sorry about earlier. I didn't mean to scare you."

Sophie couldn't hold in her chuckle. She laughed. "You didn't. I have an older brother that's a cop. He taught me how to defend myself for the most part, and Marshall taught me how to shoot. I could have protected us both, if the need arose."

"You would have shot me?" Cord's gaze slipped down to her purse and back up to Sophie's face. She watched as the knowledge settled in and he understood.

"Only in the knee to slow your big ass down." She shrugged.

His lips tilted up at the corners. "Good. That's going to make things easier."

Sophie couldn't help the confusion from showing. "Come again?"

"I'm going to help you find this asshole."

She shook her head. "I don't think that's a good idea. I think you're too emotionally invested in the situation. You won't be thinking clearly."

He took a step in her direction. His palm landed on her arm. "I know them better than any of you. I've been through everything that they own. I can help you solve this. I owe it to them and my mom. I should have been here to protect them, but I wasn't. Let me help."

Sophie glanced back up toward the house. She could see Marshall and Mrs. Reyes standing at the window, each of them watching and waiting for different reasons.

"Please." He folded his arms across his chest. "I won't tell you anything unless you let me help."

She turned back toward Cord, listening to the nagging feeling in her gut that this, too, would be a mistake. She couldn't be responsible for the woman losing another child. Not when she could do something to stop it. "You haven't even told your mom about your abilities. You aren't ready to help us." She shook her head. "I can't. Your mom needs you now and I won't be responsible for anything happening to you too. I just can't. I hope you can understand."

Sophie walked back toward the house, leaving Cord in the driveway. She pulled the door open. Her heart clenched with the knowledge that this, too, had been a wasted trip. Sophie held Marshall's gaze and nodded to the SUV.

"I'm sorry for any trouble we caused and for your loss," Sophie announced before walking back out the way she'd come. Cord was nowhere in sight.

10 CHAPTER

Sophie explained what had transpired after they left and were headed back toward the hotel. Marshall might not have agreed with her reasoning, but he didn't argue. This was the right thing to do for that family, even if it did set them back. They'd find what they needed another way. They'd have to.

Marshall guided Sophie, with his hand on her lower back, through the lobby and into the elevator.

"I would have killed him before I let him touch you," Marshall announced.

She turned to face him. "Yet it was okay that he hit you?"

"I deserved it." Marshall pressed his lips into a fine line.

"Why? Because they both died and you didn't? You didn't kill them, Marshall, and neither did Jack. You're a good man, and if I can see that, why can't you?"

"Sophie, you may think you know me, but you don't." Marshall stabbed a button and then stepped toward her, pinning her against the elevator wall, his palms planted against the wall on each side of her head. The door closed behind them.

Her heart raced, and not because she was scared.

"I'm ruthless, I'm demanding, and I go after what I want without hesitation."

"Not with me." Her voice came out a whisper.

"Especially with you." His face softened, and he trailed a finger down her face. "You're caring and loving and give of yourself without thought to how you might get hurt. I'll never let anyone hurt you."

Sophie placed her hands on his chest. She read the truth in his eyes. She believed him, and more than that, she couldn't find a reason to fight the truth. She ran her hands up his chest and behind his neck and lowered his head to meet hers. "This is going to be complicated."

His eyes softened. "We'll deal with it."

She moistened her lips.

"Are you sure?" he asked, pressing his body into hers.

His fingers tangled in her hair at the nape of her neck. She felt the beat of his heart, his erection pressed in her belly. Oh god, was she going to do this? A momentary hesitation flickered through her brain, but not long enough to dissuade her, before she pushed it away. She pressed her lips to his in a kiss that was long overdue. Her body molded against his, even as the dings of the elevator sounded in her ears. Her nipples hardened in anticipation and pressed against the hard expanse of his chest. He held her, his arms surrounding her, as their tongues met. He tilted his head for better access and pressed her harder into the wall. One hand was still in her hair and the other on her ass. Their bodies pressed intimately together as he pulled her closer, tasting her as she tasted him back. He swallowed her moan. Her kiss turned frantic as she began to want more, her need overwhelming. They forgot their surroundings until the ding of the elevator announced the arrival at their floor and the doors slid open.

He broke the kiss, his chest heaving as he fought to catch his breath. He pulled her out of the elevator and pressed her against the wall in the hallway. His forehead rested against hers, the need between them still strong. "I need a minute before we go in."

Her hands were on his hips, and she didn't move. She wasn't sure she could. She felt the electricity crackling between them. It was almost like a living thing, hot and unsteady.

He cupped her cheek and pressed a gentle kiss to her lips.

"We can't do this here," she whispered. "We need to wait until all of this is behind us."

His brows dipped. "We've waited long enough."

"Marshall..."

"I know, Sophie." He straightened and released his hold on her. "I know."

He clasped their fingers together and started walking down the hall. She lifted their hands, staring at the entangled digits. "This isn't waiting."

"Just give this to me. I need to feel you for just a few more minutes. A few more minutes until we step back into reality." He kissed the inside of her wrist before releasing her and walking into the suite.

She walked toward the fridge and pulled out a bottle of water in search of something cold to douse the flames burning inside of her. Aiden was standing in the kitchenette, leaning against the counter as Marshall disappeared into his room.

Aiden ran the pad of his thumb over her lip. "You look like a girl that's just been thoroughly kissed."

Sophie couldn't help the heat that rose to her cheeks. "Is it that obvious?"

He dropped his hand and winked. "Only to me."

He left her alone in the tiny kitchen, returning to sit on the couch with his computer in front of him. Sheets of printer paper lay on the coffee table in front of the sofa. She sat in one of the chairs and picked up a couple sheets of the paper.

"What's this?" she asked.

"Part of the alumni Ben gathered from Marshall's graduating class." He reached for another pile and handed those to her. "Here are the rest of them."

"Oh my," she exclaimed. "How many total?"

"Two hundred graduates and another seven hundred in the rest of the student body."

Sophie's mouth parted as she glanced up at Aiden. "You have a pen?"

"Sure." He tossed one to her. "What are you going to do with that?"

"Mark out the women. Macy told me that *he* would kill her if she didn't play along. We're looking for guy."

He nodded and started clicking away on the computer. "I'm trying to see what else I can find to help us narrow the list down."

"Any chance you can get their cell phone numbers and check cell towers that were used the nights of the murders? Maybe we can rule out a few people."

His brows rose. "You're brilliant. Of course, I can do that. Just as soon as I finish the financials."

"Where's Ben? Why isn't he working on those?"

Aiden nodded toward the closed bedroom door. "He's trying to hack into the television station's employees' emails and phones to see if he can get a hit on the informant. He thinks that the informant may be the killer since he's leaking the information.

"That's a great idea, but that's assuming this asshole is working alone, and we know he wasn't. He was using Macy and Janice. There's no telling who else."

Sophie started marking out the women's names, and Marshall emerged from the room thirty minutes later.

"Did you enjoy your nap, old geezer?" Aiden asked.

Marshall chuckled and squeezed Sophie's shoulder as he walked behind the couch and toward the kitchen. "I just got off the phone with Jack to tell him about the Coach, but it seems he already knew." Marshall walked back into the living room and plopped down in the recliner. He met Sophie's gaze.

"I told him while I was waiting on you guys. I called to check on him and give him updates."

Ben walked out of his bedroom, waving papers in his hand. "Seems the coroner has issued a time of death for Janice."

"Well, don't keep us in suspense."

"Eight PM the night before."

Sophie's mouth dropped open. "You mean the killer went back and hit me over the head? Why the hell would he go back to the scene of the crime?"

"Someone was there, but it may not have even been the killer," Ben explained. "Maybe he forgot something, or maybe it wasn't the killer at all, but one of his lackeys wiping the prints or something similar." He dropped the papers on the table. "Where were you that night, Sophie?"

"Eating pizza with Amber and drinking. I was in the whole night. Both Jack and Marshall stopped by shortly before that."

Ben turned his gaze to Marshall. "And where were you, boss? Do you have an alibi, or will we be providing you one?"

Marshall sat back in the recliner and crossed one leg to rest on his opposite knee. His lips tilted up in a smile. Either he had a really good alibi, or he'd figured something out.

He started laughing, picked up his phone, and sent off a text. He didn't answer them until he'd laid it back down. "I was with Jack, and even better, we can prove it."

Sophie's mouth parted. "You can? You met up with him after you left me that night?"

He nodded. "I figured he could use a friend, and it sounds like it was good thing I did."

"Where'd you go? I can try and pull up surveillance footage as proof."

"That's not necessary. I have our proof covered and it's being handled as we speak. By morning, all of us will be cleared."

Aiden clapped his hands together and rubbed them. "Great, then we can pack up and head home?"

Macy, Janice, and Ryan appeared right then, each of them standing near the blinds in the back of the room. They were waiting for the answer to the question.

"You guys can head home. I think I'm going to stay here and figure this out. We still need to catch this guy before he strikes again." Sophie frowned. "For the victims and the families."

Marshall nodded at her. "Sophie's right. We aren't done yet. We can just breathe a little easier for the time being."

Aiden began pecking at keys on the laptop again. "Then we'll press on."

They each continued with their tasks into early evening. Sophie ordered food from the diner across the street and was about to leave to go get it when someone knocked on the door. Everyone in the room turned quiet, and they all looked at her standing there with her fingers poised on the door.

"Who is it?" she asked.

"Cord Reyes. I'd like to speak with Sophie Masterson."

Sophie pulled the door open. Cord stood on the other side with an envelope stuffed beneath his arm. Marshall was standing behind her now, and the others had moved closer within sight.

"Can I speak to you?"

"Sure." She stepped back and held the door open. "Would you like to come in?"

His gaze moved throughout the room before he shook his head. "Do you mind stepping out here?"

"Not at all." Sophie grabbed her purse and looped it over her head and across her body. "We can talk while I go pick up the food."

"Sophie..." Marshall started.

She smiled at him. "It's okay, honest. You guys know I'm leaving with him, so if I don't show back up, then you'll know who has me." She patted her purse. "Besides, I've got my trusty friend."

He nodded and stepped back, not protesting any further. She entwined her arm around Cord's and led him back toward the elevators. He didn't talk until they heard the click of the suite door closing.

"How'd you find me?" she asked as they stepped into the elevator.

"It wasn't hard. It's the nicest hotel in town and I figured, with Marshall involved, you'd be in the penthouse."

"Nice detective work. I thought you weren't going to help. Why are you here?"

"I told my mother."

Sophie tilted her head. "Did she believe you?"

He shrugged. "Only when I started describing relatives I've never met. I'd say she's convinced now."

Sophie smiled. "And how does that feel to know you have a support team in place?"

"That's left to be seen," he answered as the elevator chimed their arrival to the lobby. They both stepped out and waited to finish the conversation until they made it out of the building.

"How do you figure? The closest person to you now knows. That's a good thing." She glanced at him as they walked toward the diner.

"Sophie, I want to help you find the killer, and more than that, I want you to train me."

That statement caught Sophie off guard. It was one she hadn't been expecting. "I'm still learning myself."

"Then we can learn together." He pulled the diner door open. "Just think about it, please." He grabbed the package beneath his arm and held it out to her. "This is Macy's diary and both of their yearbooks. I figured maybe if you read some of the entries, you could figure it out."

Well, the surprises just kept coming. She regarded him as she waited to pay. "Have you eaten yet?"

He shook his head.

"What do you want?"

"I always get the cheeseburger and onion rings when I come here."

"Does this place deliver?"

He nodded. She paid for the group's order and placed his before digging hers out of the bag. She handed the bag containing the men's dinners and a note she'd written on a napkin, to waitress so she could give it to the delivery boy. She generously tipped them both to have the food taken across the street. Cord and Sophie grabbed a table in the back, and she dug into her food while they waited on his.

"I don't think the others are going to like the fact that you're eating here. I don't think they trust me very much."

"They know where we went and who I'm with. If I disappear, Marshall will find me. He always does." She glanced out the window over to the top floor of the hotel across the street. She could almost feel eyes on her as she continued to eat. "I still don't want you to be a part of this investigation, whether I decide to work with you in the future or not."

Cord leaned back in the booth and waited for the waitress to set his food down before he spoke again. "I'm not going to get hurt if that's what you're worried about. I was trained by our government's finest. When I graduated, I joined the Marines, and let's just say they trained me well, in more than just fighting and shooting."

Sophie dipped a fry in her ketchup and stuffed it in her mouth. "Oh yeah? What was your specialty?"

"That's a matter of national security. I'm afraid I can't disclose that information."

Sophie grinned. She liked Cord. He was loyal to a fault and friendly and every now and then cracked a joke. She wanted to help him. She should help him. It was probably written in some divine paper somewhere that it was destiny to help him. "Fine, you can help with the crappy stuff on this one. I can already tell that the paperwork alone is going to give me a headache."

Cord grinned around his cheeseburger and continued to devour the whole thing. They talked about their abilities and how Sophie had figured out that she had them. She enjoyed talking to others who held the same interest she had about the possibilities for helping others and finding missing persons and a whole slew of other areas to help others heal. It was therapeutic finding someone like herself, someone who would understand her complaints and not just sympathize with her when they couldn't possibly understand.

They agreed she would tell the guys that night and that he'd return in the morning. He walked her back to the hotel, and she took the package with her into the elevator where he'd said goodbye. She was going to have some explaining to do, but it was for the best that she and Cord got to talk and learn a bit more about each other in a comfortable environment.

Sophie walked into an empty suite, went into her bedroom, and stashed the stuff that Cord had given her. She walked back out in the living room to find the empty food containers sticking out of the trashcan. On the counter in the kitchen was a note with her name on it.

Hey, Sophie, Ben is at the bar downstairs. I ran to the store, and Marshall was headed to the pool to swim laps.

Aiden signed the note with big X's and O's.

Neither option was appealing to her. Maybe it was the fact that she was going to have to explain to Marshall what she wanted or possibly the fact that she wanted to be sober enough to work some more that night. Regardless, she made a cup of coffee and went to sit on the couch. She picked up the school roster and continued crossing off the women's names. She left the ambiguous ones for later to compare them with the yearbooks that Cord had given her.

Sophie finished the list and started looking into the financials. She looked at the numbers until her eyes began to cross. She lay down on the couch, crossing her legs, and continued reading each large line item from the people involved, hoping that something would jump out at her. The last thing she remembered was that she was going to rest her eyes for a bit in hopes it might help her stay awake. Her eyes slid shut and she fell instantly asleep.

11 CHAPTER

Sophie rolled on the bed, snuggling into the body pressed against hers. A heartbeat pulsed beneath her palm. She snuggled closer. The smell of chlorine drifted to her nose and her eyes shot open. She glanced up at the man sleeping beside her. His big body was sprawled on the top of the covers, and he wore nothing but boxers and a T-shirt, his breathing even and steady as she continued to stare at him. Marshall's hair was mussed.

She was trying to remember how she'd gotten to bed. She was wearing her T-shirt from the day before. Her legs felt the slide of the sheets against her skin. Her jeans were gone.

Sophie eased her hand from his chest and slid slowly off the bed so she didn't wake Marshall. She grabbed some clothes and went into the bathroom for a quick shower. She pulled her hair back in a ponytail before she emerged fresh and renewed, changed into fresh clothes.

Marshall hadn't moved from his position, yet his eyes were open and his hands were beneath his head. "Good morning."

Sophie felt the heat travel to her cheeks. "Good morning." She walked to her suitcase and tossed her clothes from yesterday on top. "How did I get to bed?"

"I carried you," Marshall announced. "The couch didn't look very comfortable."

She gave an unsure nod. "And you slept in my bed, why?"

His lips turned up in a grin. "Because I wanted to wake up with you in my arms."

Marshall sat up and slid his legs over the side of the bed. "How did your impromptu meeting with Cord go?"

Sophie smiled. "It went well. He's going to help us, but I set up boundaries." She moved to sit on the bed next to Marshall. She slid her fingers through his. "I think he's going to be good for me."

"Excuse me?" Marshall asked.

"You know...another person to talk to about our abilities. I also offered him a job. He's going to be my first employee."

"You don't even know his qualifications."

"I have an idea." She shrugged. "He's big, he's gifted, and if I had to guess, he's probably just as good with a gun as he is with his fists. We'll wing the rest." She glanced up at him and batted her eyelashes. "That was okay, right?"

Marshall pulled his hand out from hers and cupped her face. "It's your department, Sophie. I trust you and your judgment." He leaned in and pressed a light kiss to her lips. "Always."

Marshall rose and walked to the door. "I'm going to go get dressed. You can tell me all about it over breakfast."

Sophie couldn't contain her smile. She wanted Marshall's approval, not only because he was her boss, but personally too.

"Hey, Marshall..." she called out before he walked out the door.

Marshall turned. "Yeah?"

"Good answer. That deserves brownie points."

Marshall laughed as he walked out her door, leaving her alone in the small room. She opened her laptop to check her emails which she hadn't touched in a few days. She clicked on one of the latest. The return address was from anonymous. The subject read: You're next. Sophie clicked it open. Photos made up the body of the email. Photos of her in the lobby, photos of her at the diner, and another of her in the pool with the others. The message beneath the pictures was, "I see you. Are you ready to play?"

Sophie stared at the computer screen, unable to move. The bastard was coming for her. She should be thrilled, yet a shiver of apprehension skirted down her spine. They were being watched.

And worse than that, not a one of them had even noticed. Was this the killer's idea of enticing her to play along?

She eased her laptop closed as her mind raced with the implications. Should she tell the others? If she did, would Marshall send her home, and what then? What if the asshole followed? It's not as though he didn't already know where she lived, where she worked, and probably even what brand of toothpaste she used. The prick.

An hour later, after they returned from breakfast, the email was still heavy on her mind. A couple of times while eating Marshall had asked if she was okay. He'd given her inquisitive looks, and yet Ben and Aiden hadn't noticed at all. She'd said she had a headache. She'd needed some excuse to go back to the room and look through the stuff that Cord had brought. She was the only one who knew it was even there and had been provided. She picked up the student list and headed toward her room. Dropping the papers on the bed, she returned to find Marshall, Ben, and Aiden getting ready to leave. Today's agenda was checking out Janice's home to look for clues. And as much as she'd wanted to go, she'd used the excuse of Cord showing up and her headache to stay behind.

A knock sounded on the door about ten minutes after the guys left.

"Who is it?"

"Cord."

She pulled the door open and let him in. She peeked up and down the hallway before she closed the door and locked it. "Are you afraid I was followed or something?"

"We were," she answered. "I haven't told the guys about this, but I've got something to show you." She walked into the bedroom and carried out her laptop. She booted it, pulled up the email, and handed him the computer.

Cord sat down beside her and scrolled through the pictures, his head tilted to the side in contemplation. "I'll be a son of a bitch. This guy knows everything."

Sophie nodded. "That was my thought. I mean, hell, he even had one of you and me at the diner."

"Why didn't you tell Marshall?"

She shrugged. "Because I know what his reaction will be. He's going to want me out of the investigation. We knew coming into this that eventually I would be a target, but I'm not ready to go yet. I'm close; I can feel it in every fiber of my being. I just need a little more time."

Ryan appeared in the room, a big broad smile on his face even though he still wasn't talking. He used both pointer fingers to direct them toward his smile.

"He's here, isn't he?" Cord asked. "I can feel him."

Sophie smiled. "Yeah, he's standing by the television." Sophie tilted her head, taking in his smile. "And what's even weirder than that is he's smiling at us."

"That's his unofficial way of communicating that we're on the right track. I've already told you that my brother will try to circumvent the system." Cord closed the email and handed the laptop back to her. "How can I help?"

"Right now I guess you could go through the student list and highlight anyone who mentioned attending the party in his yearbook. I know it's a long shot, but it's a start. I'm going to start reading through Macy's diary and then get into her yearbook. Maybe we'll notice a commonality between the three."

"What makes you think the killer is in there?"

"He has to be." Sophie pushed up from the couch and walked into the room, returning seconds later with Macy's diary. "It was someone who knew not only Marshall and Jack, but also both your sister and your brother. We're looking for a common link, and I'm hoping her diary pinpoints a motive."

Cord settled in with the list, the yearbook, and a highlighter. They worked in silence throughout the morning. She read Macy's most intimate teenage thoughts about boys, school, her teachers, and her parents. Her hopes, wishes, and dreams. Who she liked, who she hated. Everything from her first kiss to losing her virginity. She mentioned walking in to find Mark having sex with a guy, yet she didn't say who. She'd had no idea he was gay.

It wasn't a shock she crushed on her brother's friends. She liked Jack the best, but there were quite a few entries about Marshall and Ben too. It was almost as if she couldn't decide. Like it did for many young girls, it switched based on whichever one was nicest to her and showed her more attention. She kept her crush a secret, only sharing it with her best friend, Dana. There were several entries in her diary about this girl Dana. It seemed as if they'd continued to keep in touch even through adulthood, where Macy made mention that she'd given up on writing in the antiquated book and had switched to a computer. Sophie flipped through the rest of the empty pages and paused on inside of the back cover. Written in blue ink was a number with an area code from Sophie's hometown. The initials RB were written above it.

An hour later, Sophie closed the diary, took it back to her room, and put it on the bedside table. She took the pages of names that Cord had finished with, and using another highlighter, she placed a checkmark by the names from the diary. Depending on the computer entries they still needed to find, it narrowed the list down to thirty different people for them to check out. It was everyone who'd signed the yearbook. Marshall, Jack, Ben, and Mark were on the list.

Cord capped the highlighter and set it down. "Now what?"

Sophie walked into the kitchen, grabbed two water bottles from the fridge, and tossed one to

Cord. "I was reading her diary, and she mentioned that she tells her best friend everything."

"Dana," Cord confirmed.

"Does she still live around here?"

"As a matter of fact, she does. Care to take a road trip with me?"

"That sounds perfect. Let me grab my purse and leave a note."

Sophie went into the room and grabbed her purse. When she turned around to leave, Will was standing in her path.

"What are you doing here?"

"Watching," he answered casually, his gaze following where she'd moved the diary. "You might want to take that with you."

Sophie paused. "Why?"

He shrugged. "For safekeeping. You missed something." He popped away and immediately popped back in as she went to grab the diary.

"Now you can't say I never helped you." His grin grew, and his eyes glistened with mischief before he disappeared again.

Sophie left a note for the guys that she was going to grab some lunch with Cord and that she'd be back in a bit. She bit her lip while debating on saying more and then thought better of it.
****

Cord and Sophie sat across from each other in a diner similar to the one across from the hotel, only this one was across town and a bit empty for a lunch crowd. A petite brunette walked over to the table with an order pad and pen in hand.

"What can I get ya?" she asked before even looking up.

"How are you, Pigtails?" Cord asked with a big smile.

The waitress snapped her gaze up to meet his. "No one calls me that anymore."

"I still do."

"Oh my god. Cord. You're home." Excitement lit up her face before glancing to Sophie before returning her gaze to Cord. "New girlfriend? Wife?"

"Just a friend. Do you have a second to sit and talk? It's about Macy."

The woman's smile fell. Her name tag indicated her name was Dana. "I still can't believe she's gone."

Cord scooted over, took her by the hand, and pulled her down to sit next to him in the booth before doing the introductions. "Sophie is a detective. She's trying to find Macy's killer and an explanation for Ryan's death, and I think she wants to ask you some questions."

Dana glanced to the coffee counter and beyond to the kitchen before she agreed. "We have to make it quick, or I'll get in trouble."

"When was the last time you saw Macy?" Sophie asked, diving right in. If her time was limited, she was going to make the best of it.

"I work three jobs, so it's hard to find time to socialize, but the last time I saw her was in passing on Main Street. I was late for work, but I stopped to talk to her for a quick second."

"Yeah? Do you remember what about?"

"She was going out of town and she was excited about it. She said one of her wishes was coming true."

"Did she tell you what that wish was?" Cord asked.

Dana's face reddened as she glanced at Cord and then back to Sophie. "A guy she was crushing on asked her to go away with him." Dana crushed her lips together as if debating to continue. She kept glancing at Cord under her lashes. The longer she did, the redder her face became.

"Hey, Cord. Do you think you can go get my purse out of the car?"

He gave her a quizzical look before he scooted out of the booth and pulled the keys from his pocket. She waited until the bell above the door chimed announcing his departure before she continued.

"He promised to fulfill one of her fantasies for a threesome." Dana glanced back out the window and leaned forward. "She liked girls and guys. I don't think her brother knew."

Sophie gave a slow nod. She knew that from the club, but Dana wouldn't have known that.

"Did she tell you who invited her?"

Dana shrugged. "No, I think she was too embarrassed to say because it would have hurt his reputation. All she said was it was a long time coming."

Sophie leaned back in the booth and let out a lengthy sigh. "Anyone you can think of she crushed on more than the others? Someone she would have dropped what she was doing and left town with?"

Dana visibly swallowed. "She liked the football players. As a little girl she used to tell me she was going to marry one. But we were just kids. She liked all kinds of guys and girls growing up. They weren't all jocks, although most were."

"Did she tell you Mark Campbell was gay?"

Dana nodded.

"Who was he dating, do you know?"

"If I tell you, you have to swear you won't tell a soul."

Sophie leaned closer. "I promise."

"Ben Winters. She caught Mark and Ben having sex in the photography's dark room at school."

Sophie's mouth dropped open as she leaned back in the booth; the new information was a game changer. Had Ben or even Mark been trying to off Jack for the spot on the team and if the two were in a relationship, what did it mean when Mark was sent away. Oh crap. She hadn't seen this coming.

The chime above the door rang again, and Dana pinched her lips together. "Macy and I were supposed to meet up when she got back into town to tell me how it all went, but I never heard from her." She frowned. "I guess we know why now."

Cord walked over the back of the booth chair slid in next to Sophie.

"Is there anything else you can think of? Anywhere she would have written down the information?"

Dana gave a slow shake of the head. "No."

Sophie pulled out one of her business cards and handed it to Dana. "Will you call me if you remember anything else?"

Dana slid out of the booth and shoved the card in her apron. "Sure. Can I get you two something to eat?"

Cord ordered, and Sophie ordered the same. The cheeseburger with the onion rings. He waited until Dana left before moving to the other side of the booth. He leaned forward and whispered. "What was all that about?"

"Stuff she didn't want Macy's big brother hearing," Sophie answered, and then she paused when Dana brought them some drinks. "She was enticed out of town by one of her crushes, but she didn't tell Dana who. We need to figure that out and we'll know who killed her."

"How are we going to figure that out?"

"We've been through her diary and you went through the school list. What's left to check? Do you think your mom would mind if I took a look in her room?"

"Not at all."

They ate and threw around ideas on who it could be and why. She pulled out his sister's diary from her purse, turned to the last page, and pointed to the number written there. "Do you know whose number that is?"

He shook his head. "No, but a simple check on the Internet should tell us."

"Why wait?" Sophie's eyes lit up as she walked over to the counter with the book. She tossed a few dollars on the counter and asked Dana if she could use the diner's phone.

Dana pointed her to a phone at the end of the bar and Sophie thanked her. She dialed the number listed, hoping beyond anything else that a killer or someone with her next clue would answer.

The phone rang three times before it was answered.

"Rivers," a woman answered. When Sophie didn't say anything, the female continued. "Hello?"

"I'm sorry. Who is this?" Sophie asked, hoping that the woman wouldn't counter with, "Who might you be?"

"Rivers Lowell. Who's this?"

"Rivers Lowell from Channel 7?" Sophie asked.

"Yes...who's speaking, please?"

"Tell me Ms. Lowell, why would a dead young woman have your number?"

"Who is this?" Rivers asked, her voice lower.

"Sophie Masterson."

"Oh my, Ms. Masterson. I just did a piece on your boyfriend and his dead girlfriend."

"I guess you also know that your piece was unfounded and I'm tempted to sue you and the station for slander. I'm sure that Monroe and Monroe would be happy to take my case, and between me and you, Alexis Monroe is a bitch. I'm sure she'd chew you up and spit you out."

"We went by the information that was provided."

"You should have checked your sources. Maybe she'll be able to add negligence to the long list of charges in the suit. And I'm sure the police would be interested to know that Macy Reyes was in contact with you. They may even find evidence that you knew of the murders and pin the role of accomplice on you personally."

"You wouldn't dare."

Sophie steeled her voice. "I'll do more than dare, Ms. Rivers. I'll make sure your career and credibility are destroyed by the time I'm finished with you. Enjoy your freedom while you can, Ms. Rivers."

"Wait...wait..." Rivers let out a lengthy exhale. "What do you want, Sophie?"

"I want your informant."

"Macy was my informant."

"Try again, Rivers," Sophie demanded. "Macy wasn't alive to give you all of the information on Janice and Jack. Who else is feeding you this crap?"

"How do I know you still won't come after me and the station?"

"You don't. After I hang up, the next time you hear from me will be through my lawyer. You have ten seconds to decide, and the clock is ticking."

"Winters. Ben Winters. He's the one sending me emails."

Sophie's heart stopped beating. The picture was becoming clearer. Why the hell would he do it? She still needed that answer before she accused the guy of killing. She needed his motive.

"You're lying," Sophie spat through gritted teeth. "I'm calling my attorney and your network."

"Just because you don't like the answer doesn't mean I'm lying, Sophie. I have proof. I have the emails and I recorded the calls."

Sophie's legs turned to jelly. She leaned against the counter to hold her weight before she ended up on her butt. Every chest heaved with every breath. "Ms. Lowell, here's what I want you to do. I need you to listen and listen well. His first objective will be to destroy the incriminating evidence and then anyone and everyone who knows where you're getting the information. There is no amount of security or bodyguards that can keep Ben away from you. He may appear to be a regular guy, but he's not. The military has trained him, and with his technical abilities, he's coming for you. It's just a matter of time."

"What the hell do you mean he's coming for me?"

"Trust me. You've made his list. Here's what I want you to do. This man is a genius with electronics. I want you to print the emails and copy whatever proof you have. Take them somewhere safe. Somewhere that he'll never be able to reach.

Nowhere in cyberspace and nowhere he'd ever imagine looking."

"Where the hell do you suppose that is?"

"Take them to my neighbor. I'll let her know you're bringing her a package and for her to hold it for me."

"Okay, then what?"

"Go to the ATM, take out as much cash as you need to leave town. Take someone with you so that you can put the hotel in someone else's name. Pay with cash when you get there. I want you to call me in two hours and ask for an exclusive. We'll have that conversation, and then you'll ditch your phone and head out of town. I'll take care of the rest. When the time is right, I'm going to need you to acknowledge that he's the one. I want you to text your new number to…. hang on…" Sophie covered the phone. "Cord, what's your cell number?"

"555-769-3456," he hollered back.

Sophie repeated the number. "It won't take long for my plan to come together. I'm thinking two days tops. I'll text you when it's over and safe for you to return."

"You want me to go off the air for two days? Are you crazy?" Rivers asked.

"Your life depends on it. Trust me, Rivers. I'll text you my number from my friend's phone, so that you'll have the number to call in two hours."

"Fine, but I want the exclusive."

"You won't believe it when I tell you all of the facts, but it's yours." Sophie hung up the phone and took a minute to collect herself. She'd just committed herself to revealing she was a clairvoyant to the world or, technically, at least the entire Channel 7 viewing area. What was she going to tell Cord? She couldn't get his help without telling him why and who was involved.

Sophie took a deep breath, dropped a few more bills on the counter to cover the length of her call, and walked back to the booth. Cord's look of anticipation matched Sophie's level of dread. There was no way this could go well. No way that she could tell Cord the entire story. Sophie needed more information. Why the hell would Ben do it? She needed more information to tie Ben with Macy and Ryan, and there was only one person who could give it to her. And he was sitting across from her.

Sophie took her phone out of her purse and shot off two texts. One to the reporter and one to Marshall, telling him that she'd be back within the hour and they needed to talk.

"Well....Who answered?"

Sophie took a sip of her drink and held the diary close to her chest. "A reporter."

Sophie reached across the table and laid her hand over Cord's. "Will you trust me to finish this? Trust that I'm making the right choices on how to proceed?"

His brow rose.

"I've set up a trap." She scrunched her nose. "Well sort of. But with your help, we can bury this guy."

"Who is it?"

"I'm afraid if I told you that you'd kill him, and I can't chance that happening. I need your help, but without the name. Can you do that? If not, I understand, but that's where I'm at."

"Are you fucking kidding me? You know who he is and you won't tell me?" Cord growled.

"I know this is hard. Probably one of the hardest things you'll ever do. But I can't have you killing the guy and going to jail yourself. I won't be responsible for taking away your mom's last child."

Cord lurched back in his seat. His silence was deafening. His help was going to be critical. There were others she could call, but they too, would want Ben dead, and what if he wasn't working alone. What if Mark was involved? Shit.

"Think of your mom," Sophie pleaded. Ryan appeared in the seat next to Cord. Cord lurched, and his eyes widened as if he could see his brother. His sister, Macy, appeared on his other side. He turned, his eyes still the size of saucers. Sophie saw the goose bumps on his arms. He was not only aware of his siblings; he could see them.

"She's right," Ryan announced.

"She's lost too much. Don't make her lose you too," Macy said.

Cord's eyes turned glassy. He closed his eyes, and when he opened them, a tear slipped free, and his brother and sister were gone.

"Well, I guess you can see them now, and they aren't restricted from talking to you," Sophie said to lighten the mood. "Think of it like this... We all have this grand path, and I plan on doing a crap load of good. One way to decide is to figure out if your love for your mom and siblings outweighs your hate."

"That's crap, Sophie, and you know it."

"I need to trust you. I need to trust that if you work with me that you'll have my back, no matter how much you'd rather take vengeance into your own hands. If you can't do it, tell me now. I'm still going to get this guy. It's just a matter of whether you'll be helping." She glanced down at her watch. "I've got one hour before she's going to call me, and I have a lot to do before then. I need an answer. I'll understand if you tell me no."

Cord let out a long breath. He tilted his head. "You'll see this through to the end? You swear this guy won't get off on a technicality?"

She shook her head. "No technicality for him. Now that I know who he is, this ends with us."

His gaze searched hers, as if looking for answers. "Fine. What do you need me to do?"

"How good are you with a gun?" She asked with a grin.

"I'm an expert with all weapons, and not to boast, but I can hold my own against hackers too." He answered.

"I need you to fly to Easton. Set up my townhouse so that I'll have weapons stashed everywhere, yet out of sight. Most importantly, I want it wired with video and sound to be recorded and saved off site and sent to my brother at the police department." She took a long breath. "Can you do that? Do you even know how to do that?"

Cord's lips tilted up in a grin. "I can do that in my sleep."

"Some of that super-secret-I'll-have-to-kill-you-if-I-tell-you stuff?"

He chuckled. "Yep."

"Well, there's more to it."

"Oh?" He crossed his arms on the table. "More than everything you just asked for?"

"Yeah, this is the scary part. Are you sure you're up to it?"

His brows dipped. "Hit me with it."

"You get to stay with my neighbor and monitor everything in the event this jerk kills me. I need to make sure the video feed gets in the hands of the authorities."

"Who's your neighbor?"

Sophie smiled. "A seventy-five-year-old woman who will probably flirt with you. She's the quintessential busybody of the neighborhood."

"If she'll have me, I'll be there."

Sophie laid some cash on the table and rose. "You've got to get me to the hotel, and I need you to go to the airport. The pilot will be expecting you."

"Really?"

"Really."

Sophie brushed her hair out of her face when they stepped outside. The wind from the approaching hurricane had picked up just in the short time they were inside. She got in Cord's car and started making the appropriate preparations on the way back to the hotel. After calling the pilot and requesting the flight, she also planned that he come right back and pick them up while the weather held up. Cord dropped her off and was heading to the airport as she waved goodbye.

She had some explaining to do and only a little time left to do it before the phone call was supposed to take place. She took a deep breath and walked into the hotel lobby. Her eyes scanned the area as she headed for the elevator. Her heart raced as she clutched her purse closer to her body, the press of the gun her only sources of safety. She was walking into the killer's web. Easy access was an understatement. She wouldn't be sleeping tonight.

12 CHAPTER

Sophie took the elevator up to the top floor and headed for their suite. She pulled her card key out of her pocket and walked in like nothing had changed. All was okay. She made eye contact with Marshall immediately. His brows dipped in question. He didn't have any idea what was going on, but before tonight was over, he would.

She held his gaze and gave him a slight shake of her head. He gave a slight nod that no one would have noticed had they not been looking for it.

"Where have you been all day?" Aiden asked.

"Checking out a few leads with my new employee." She walked into the kitchenette, grabbed bottled water, and took a sip to coat her dry throat. "What have you guys been doing all day?"

"We checked Janice's house and talked to a few of her friends."

Sophie's brow rose. "How'd that work out for you? Anything new to report?"

"Nope. Her house was completely empty. We're still looking to where her things might be."

Sophie plopped down on the edge of the recliner where Marshall was sitting. He rubbed small circles on her back. Ben was in the other chair and Aiden was perched on the couch.

"Any hits on the financials, Ben?"

He shook his head. "Nothing out of the ordinary for anyone."

"Damn, I thought that was going to be a lead. Well, I have a lead…" She stood, walked into her bedroom, and grabbed the yearbook and list they'd complied. She tossed everything on the coffee table on top of the papers. "These are Macy and Ryan's yearbooks. I've narrowed our suspect list down to thirty potentials, not counting you two and Jack, of course."

Sophie retook her spot on the armrest of Marshall's chair, and her phone vibrated. She grabbed it out of her pocket, checked the caller ID, and held in her grin. She answered, "Masterson."

"Hey. It's me. Set your stage."

"Why would I give you an exclusive, Ms. Rivers? You've got to be crazy. You tried to destroy my repetition, not to mention Jack's. Why would I even think about talking to you?"

Sophie paused for effect, even though there was only dead air. Everyone paused in what they were doing, every gaze pinned on her.

"You will?" She turned to face Marshall, covered the receiver with her hand and whispered, "She's going to give me her informant."

"Her informant has to be the killer. He knows too much."

Sophie's eyes widened and she smiled. "Yep." She uncovered the phone. "Yes. I'll give you an exclusive if you give me your informant."

Sophie walked over to the bar blocking off the kitchen and grabbed a pen and paper. "Tomorrow, 6 PM at my house. My address is 315 Pembrook Drive." She wrote down the appointment and dropped the pen on the pad and turned around. "Great. I'll see you then."

Sophie hung up the phone with a big grin on her face. "It looks like tomorrow night we'll have a name to turn over to the police."

"Great. But you aren't doing this alone."

Sophie walked to him and sat back down. "You can come, but I don't want a full team there. I don't want to scare the reporter away."

"Agreed," Marshall answered.

"Just you and me."

"Just you and me," he confirmed.

Sophie stood and walked into her room and into her bathroom. She closed the door and leaned back against the wood. Her heart raced. Bile rose to her throat. She'd done some crazy things in the past, but this ranked up with the craziest of them all.

Knuckles rapped against the door.

"Soph," Marshall whispered. "Are you okay?"

She opened the door and glanced toward her open bedroom door. She whispered, "I need to talk to you, but not here and not now."

Marshall leaned against the doorframe. "Where do you want to go?"

"Take me for a drive and show me where you grew up."

Marshall's lips tilted up in a smile. "Perfect."

He moved out of the way and let Sophie lead. "Ben, I need the keys. I'm going to take Sophie on a tour."

Ben tossed him the keys.

"Pack up, guys. We're leaving in the morning. It seems Sophie and I have a meeting to attend," Marshall announced while picking up her purse and handing it to her.

Sophie waited until they were outside in the car and headed down the road before she pulled out the diary and set it on her lap. "Cord brought me Macy's diary, and even though there were lots of names and crushes that I used to pare down the list, it wasn't until we went to the diner to meet her best friend that I was informed why Macy was in town to begin with."

Marshall glanced at her as he drove. "You found out why she was there?"

"Don't tell Cord, but Macy wanted a threesome, and someone she trusted offered her the opportunity."

Marshall's brows rose when he glanced at her again. "Well, I'd say that was correct. We saw her with both men and women at the club the night she died. So who enticed her?"

"That's going to have to wait until you find us a place to park. I have a story to tell and what I did when I learned the information. I need you focused and not behind the wheel."

He looked at her, his brows dipped, his jaw set. "Fine."

He accelerated a bit faster as he drove through the town and turned on a country road, similar to Cord's. He continued up the road until they came to a one-story old house with no cars in the drive. The small house had a pond off to the side.

Marshall parked and took a deep breath. "Come on."

He got out and walked up to the house. He inserted a key into the lock and twisted the knob.

"Where are we?"

"The house I grew up in."

"You kept it?"

"Of course I did. It's got sentimental memories." He walked into the house and flicked on the light switch. What she'd expected was a thick layer of dust over everything and to be

KATE ALLENTON

sneezing when she walked in. She turned in place. Everything was clean and kept up. There wasn't a dust bunny in sight.

"You have a maid."

"You could say that." He chuckled as they entered the living room.

"Can I borrow her?"

He smiled, and the light in his eyes sparkled. It was a shame what she had to tell him was going to make that light diminish. "You're stalling."

"You're observant. You want to have a seat."

He shook his head and crossed his arms over his chest. "Tell me."

She held out her hand. "Give me your phone."

He tilted his head. "Why do you want my phone?"

"Because I know you. I need you calm to help me deal with this."

"That bad?"

"Worse than you could think."

Marshall handed over his phone and Sophie stuffed it into her purse so they wouldn't forget it. "There was a phone number in the diary, so I called it."

"And?"

"It was the reporter. I guess you could say I convinced her to tell me who her informant was."

"How did you do that?"

"Threatened a lawsuit, prosecution, and destruction of her reputation and career."

Marshall chuckled. "You're learning. What did she say?"

Sophie swallowed around the softball-sized lump in her throat. Her stomach rolled in protest. "Not only did she give me a name, but she said she has proof."

"Sophie, quit stalling."

She took a deep breath. "Ben Winters. She has emails and messages that she saved." Her shoulders sagged. "It was Ben. I haven't figured out if he's working alone or if Mark Campbell is in on it, but I will."

Marshall's arms dropped to his side, his hands balled into fists, his look deadly. "I'll kill the bastard. Do you want to explain the phone call from the reporter?"

She plopped down in a chair. "A set-up. I want him to come after me, which we both know he'll do."

"Have you lost your fucking mind?" He growled. "He will kill you, Sophie. He's more than an IT guy. He's vicious and ruthless, and he's trained." Marshall threw his hands up. "You have to call it off. I'll take him down, not you."

She eased to perch on the edge of the chair. "It's too late."

"No, it's not. You can have another phone call with the reporter. Call the damn thing off."

She shook her head. "I've already sent Cord ahead of us. He's wiring my house and planting weapons. I'm going to get the bastard to confess and send it to the cops. That's the only way that Macy and Ryan will get justice."

Marshall walked over to her and crouched down in front of her. "You aren't doing this."

"I am doing this." She nodded. "I'll have you with me, and Cord will be at the neighbor's recording everything. He's stashing weapons, cameras, and audios as soon as he lands."

"You sent him in the plane?"

She took his hands in hers. "I had no other choice. I needed to get him there in time to set up everything."

"I'm going to kill Ben."

She shook her head. "No, you're not. We have to figure out if he was working alone."

"We have to plan," he announced, rising to stand in front of her, his crotch at eye level. Even in the pit of despair when friends turn into enemies and enemies turn into friends, her desire for Marshall didn't waver. Her hands itched to grab him, to hold him. Her heart raced with the need to make love with him.

She rose to stand in front of him. Her palms pressed against his chest; she slid them up to lock her fingers behind his neck.

"Show me your room." Sophie's voice came out a whisper.

"You're trying to distract me."

"Yes. I am." She chewed on her bottom lip and rubbed her arms back down his chest. "Is it working?"

"We need to deal with this."

She pulled his head down, his lips a mere inch from hers. "We will. Just not right now."

Marshall swept Sophie up in his arms and held her pressed against his rock-hard chest and then walked down the dark hall. Was she really going to sleep with Marshall? When she did, there would be no going back. No time travelling invention to undo what she'd done.

"I can walk," she announced.

"I know," he answered.

Marshall opened the bedroom door without setting her down and stepped into an even darker space. He kicked the door closed behind him.

Marshall followed her down to lie on the soft mattress before he reached over and flicked the bed-side lamp on.

Sophie leaned up on her elbows, ignoring his wandering hands. Her lips tilted up in a smile. "I expected some centerfolds on the wall or even a teen poster of a role model or your favorite sports team." She glanced at him. "I wasn't expecting this."

Marshall lay down on the bed and cupped his hands behind his head. "There's nothing wrong with a healthy appetite for boats."

She turned to look at him. "Do you have one?"

He nodded. "Yes."

"Do you find time to enjoy it?"

He shrugged. "I've never been on it."

Sophie's mouth parted. "Why bother if you don't go on it? Is it a guy thing? I'm man. I need a boat to catch fish." Her lips tilted up in a smile. "You're a closet hoarder, aren't you? First the weapons and now a boat. What's next, mansions?"

"Hardly." He chuckled. "This was my grandfather's study before I came to live with them. Before the accident, they were going to buy a boat and sail around the world." He looked around the room with what looked like appreciation. "They gave up those plans to raise my sister and me. The least I could do was respect their dreams."

Sophie placed her arm across his chest and made circular patterns on the material of his shirt. "Marshall?"

He slid his arm beneath her head and pulled her closer to him. She snuggled into the crook of his arm. "Hmm?"

"What if this doesn't work?"

"I told you to call it off."

She patted at his chest. "The trap will work. That wasn't what I was talking about." She propped up on one elbow to look him in the eyes. "What if we sleep together and we find out later we aren't compatible? We have to work with each other. It's going to be hard to see you every day after everything that happens."

Marshall chuckled and pulled her back down to lie with him. "Sophie, you're breaking us up before we even have a chance to start."

"I'm worried."

Marshall ran his hands through Sophie's hair. "About what, baby?"

"I'm worried a relationship and sleeping together will ruin everything."

He turned so they lay face to face. "Or it will make it better."

"Or I'll be jobless and heartbroken."

"Or you'll be loved for the rest of my life. Marry me, Sophie. I'll never break your heart."

"Marshall, be serious."

"I am. Think of the perks. You'll get to sleep with me every night. You'll have someone to make your coffee every morning. We'll get to share the daily commute, and I'll even throw in a new boat." He grinned.

"And what would you get in return?" She smiled. The tension in her shoulders eased. "You'd get a wife that talks to dead people, the same woman who finds trouble everywhere she goes. And let's save the best reason why we shouldn't for last." She leaned forward on her elbow. Her brows pulled together as the realization just hit her. She pressed a tiny kiss to his lips. "Your best friend would disown you, and that would break my heart. Those are all the reasons why you shouldn't want to marry me." She shook her head. "Talk about putting the cart before the horse."

She pushed all thoughts of Jack out of her mind. She was with Marshall. She was committed to exploring the chemistry between them. She'd made her choice, and she would stick with it.

She leaned against his chest and pressed a firmer kiss to his lips. He'd let her deepen the kiss and take what she wanted, only she could sense his hesitation. She could feel it. He wasn't a man on the verge of losing control. He was something altogether different. She broke the kiss to look into his eyes.

"What's wrong?"

Marshall gritted his teeth and clenched his eyes shut as he slid off the bed to stand. He faced her. A decision had been made, yet he hadn't clued her in on what that was.

"What?" she asked again.

"No sex, until you say yes."

Sophie's mouth parted, and she stared at him, momentarily stunned. What the hell did he mean no sex? She'd been looking forward to exploring that pleasure with him.

"Yes to what...exactly?" she asked hesitantly.

"Until we're married."

"You can't be serious."

"I'm saving your virtue."

She couldn't help the bubble of laughter that escaped her lips. "My virtue sailed a long time ago when I was a teen. You missed that boat."

He shook his head. His lips pressed in a fine line. "I'm serious, Sophie."

She tilted her head; an evil grin split her lips. "What are you going to do in the meantime?"

"Abstain," he answered without thought. During the time he stood there, he apparently decided to amend his decision. "Well…I'll deal with it myself." He nodded as if sure of his decision. "We're going to date."

Sophie held up her hand. "Whoa…. didn't agree to this. What if I want to have sex?"

He grinned. "I think you women refer to the substitute as Bob. Do I need to stock you up on batteries?"

Her grin returned, even bigger than before. "No…I think I have plenty. I may even let you watch."

She slid off the other side of the bed, trying to hide the aggravation from her face as he moved to her side. He stood mere inches from her, his words whispered against her lips. "So you don't forget what it is we're waiting for."

The air was charged with their desire as they stared into one another's eyes. Energy crackled along Sophie's skin, setting her nerve endings on fire. Heat pulsed in her veins, leaving her throbbing with need. She ached for him, for his touch, his kiss.

She watched Marshall's head lower, her gaze fastened on his lips. His breath teased her as he closed the gap between them. Heart thundering in her chest, her body swayed toward him.

Marshall's hands curled around her biceps, pulling her lush curves tight against his hard frame. His scent surrounded her, pulled her in, the spice of his cologne sending a shiver down her spine. Sophie's lips parted, and her eyes drifted shut. She heard her blood roaring in her ears as time stood still. And then his lips met hers.

His kiss was raw, savage, as he demanded more from her. The taste of him exploded on her tongue. Her thighs clenched to stave off the growing ache between her legs. She felt moisture gather at her core. Her hands fisted his shirt as she clung to him, needing him now more than ever before. Marshall's tongue dipped, swirled, and tangled with hers in a sensual mating dance that left her knees weak and made her tremble in his arms.

She felt the rasp of his five o'clock shadow against her delicate skin, and the thought of those whiskers caressing her in other places, more intimate places, had her pressing her body against him. Her nipples, peaked with need, ached. It was all she could do not to plead with him, beg him, to take them in his mouth and suck long and hard on each rosy tip.

As his tongue plunged into her mouth again, she clenched her legs tighter together to ease her throbbing. Her channel clenched and unclenched, needing to be filled, stretched, and claimed. And Marshall was claiming her, in the only way he'd promised. A kiss so earth-shattering, so explosive, so passionate that he'd leave her aching for more. Was that his plan, a need that would go unfulfilled? A simple yes would be enough, yet she couldn't say it. It left her feeling raw, the walls around her heart refusing to give him what he desired to satisfy her craving. It was war. He was on one side of the line and she on the other. It was a battle of wills to see who would surrender first. A test of desires, a reminder of the sexy, steamy possibilities.

His kiss gentled, slowed, and then he pulled away. His hooded eyes were dark with desire. Sophie panted, wondering why he'd stopped, yet thankful that he had. She smoothed her hands up his chest and slid them around his neck, intent on drawing him back down for another taste, but he held firm, resolute.

"Say yes."

"No." She cleared her throat. "And that wasn't very nice."

He shrugged, one side of his lips tilted at the corner. "I go after what I want without reservation. You know that."

She took a step back to distance them, to curb the energy between them. "Well, if you aren't going to give me any, then I suggest we get to plotting."

Marshall slid his fingers between hers and guided her back down the hall to a safer part of the house. If they'd stayed in the bedroom, she might have ripped his clothes off, just to prove her point that her will was stronger and would outlast his.

They reached the living room, and he grabbed his keys off the counter and held out his hand. "Can I have my phone back?"

She picked up her purse and pulled out his phone, holding it out of his reach. "We don't know if he's working with anyone else, so you can't call anyone else in to help."

He cornered her against the counter, his breath hot on her neck as he slid his phone out of her hand. She let him. "I know. Your plan is good, but it needs a little tweaking." He kissed her neck and stepped back. "Where is Cord staying?"

"With my neighbor."

Marshall's laughter filled the hallway as they left the tiny house he'd grown up in and got into the SUV to go back to the hotel and spend the night with a killer.

"I'm staying in your room."

She shrugged. "Don't you think they might find that unusual since we haven't shared the same room since we arrived?"

"I've slept in your room once." He started the SUV and backed down the drive. "When you fell asleep on the couch." He stopped at the end of the gravel path, put the SUV into drive, and started back the way they'd come.

"It's going to be hard to act normal around him until we get the evidence."

He slid his fingers through hers and gave a gentle squeeze to her hand. "You'll never be alone with him."

"I guess that means we're showering together?" She chuckled.

He glanced her way, a grin on his face. "We'll think of something."

They rode back in a comfortable silence together, yet her nerves were on edge. Not because of Marshall's closeness or the grip of his hand or even the way he was rubbing the outside of her thumb. Her nerves were wrestling with all of the things that could go wrong tonight and tomorrow. She'd tried to plan and be prepared. She would be ready, Cord would be ready, and Marshall would be by her side. She had everything she needed. Didn't she? Her life was the only factor riding on being ready when Ben showed up at her house. If he actually showed. The asshole had better show.

13 CHAPTER

Sophie shoved her key into her lock, glad to be home and yet nervous as hell. Ben hadn't made a move the night before. Sleep had eluded her, and her body remained fatigued, the shower doing nothing to ease the knots in her muscles. Today was D-day. The day when she reclaimed her life and brought justice to the fallen. Today was the day that would remind her why she was doing this.

She stepped into her dark house and paused, seeing the large figure standing in the dark. She could just make out the outline of his six-foot frame, but it wasn't until she heard his voice that she knew it was Cord.

"How was your flight?" he asked.

"Uneventful." She flipped the foyer light on, which he promptly flipped right back off. "Keep it off. I have some things to show you."

A chill skirted down Sophie's spine. "How am I going to see them in the dark?"

"You need to be prepared for anything. It's possible he'll cut the power to disorient you."

Cord stepped around her. He guided her fingers to the foyer table and pulled open the drawer. He ran her fingers over the gun and down toward the trigger. His body was pressed against her back. "If he attacks when you open the door, this is the closest."

He guided her down the hall, his arm around her waist as he led her. He stopped next to the recliner and reached her hand between the cushion and the back of the chair. "Number 2, if he comes at you from behind."

He rubbed her fingers over the gun and guided her to the handle so she could get a feel for how she needed to grip it.

He led her next to the couch and eased her on the end farthest away from the chair. He eased her down to sit on his lap and led her hand down between the cushion and the frame. "Number 3, if the bastard attacks while you're defenseless and sitting down."

He eased her up and proceeded to show her, in the dark, where all of the other weapons were stashed. All inconspicuous but all of the places were covered no matter where she might be standing in her house. Next to her bed. In the bathroom. In the kitchen, hell, even in her fridge and pantry. There wasn't a room or even a corner of a room that was left unprepared.

When he was done, he led her back down the hall into the living room. A tall figure was standing in front of the open back door. Before she could even remember where the nearest weapon was, the figure flinched, letting the moonlight touch his face. Marshall had his gun drawn and pointed at her and Cord.

Cord, in return, had pulled his and had the red laser pointer directed at Marshall's heart while pushing Sophie behind him, blocking her with his body.

"Shit. I thought I was too late," Marshall exclaimed as he closed the back door and walked in. "Why are the lights off?"

"Giving her direction where the weapons are stashed so she can protect herself in the dark, if the asshole cuts the power."

"Smart." Marshall turned on the lamp closest to him and closed the blinds. "Where did you learn this?"

Sophie walked into the kitchen, answering Marshall's question as she walked. "He won't tell me specifics due to national security."

She grabbed a bottle of water before returning to the room. The testosterone in the air thickened while the two men stared each other down. What the hell had happened in the two seconds she was gone?

"I know how you guys like to see who's bigger. Feel free to whip them out. I'll be the judge."

Cord's mouth dropped open, his eyes bulged. Marshall tossed his head back, laughing.

"That wasn't a joke," Sophie announced, keeping a straight face. When had she turned into a hussy when, just days ago, she wouldn't sleep with Marshall? What had changed?

Marshall moved to stand behind her. He put his arm around her waist, pulling her back against his chest. He pressed a lingering kiss against her neck and her knees almost buckled. "Play nice, baby. Do you need another reminder?"

"Yes...yes I do," she announced and turned around, waiting for a kiss that would make her forget where she was.

Her cell phone interrupted the foreplay, and she walked to the foyer and grabbed it out of her purse. She pressed it to her ear as the guys discussed where the weapons were stashed.

"Masterson."

"Did you think I was stupid?" Ben asked. "Did you think I wouldn't know?"

Sophie's heart raced, beating against her rib cage. "How?"

"It doesn't matter how. What matters is who I've got keeping me company since I got back. If Marshall even suspects you're talking to me, I'll kill her."

Her? There were only two hers that mattered most in Sophie's world, and she'd die for both of them.

"Who?" Sophie walked into the kitchen; her head drooped forward while clasping the kitchen counter to hold herself up.

"Sophie, I'm so sor—" Amber screamed in the phone before her voice cut out.

"You fucking bastard." Sophie heard Beau yell in the background before he, too, went silent.

Sophie crumbled to her knees. He had them both. This wasn't happening. This couldn't be happening.

"I'll kill you," Sophie growled through gritted teeth.

"You can try. Stand up, Sophie," Ben demanded, and she knew she was in even deeper shit than she thought. Somehow this asshole had hacked into her feed. The same feed that was supposed to take his ass out. Sophie pushed herself up and leaned against the counter.

"If you want to see your friend alive, you'll do exactly what I say. Pretend you're on the phone with your brother."

She played along. "Max, I told you I was going out of town. You could have called my cell."

"Good....now listen carefully to me. I want you to get the proof the reporter has and bring it to me."

"Sure, Max. I'll make it a point to visit Eileen in the morning," Sophie said, not trusting herself to turn toward Marshall, without her look giving her panic away.

"How am I going to get away from them?" she whispered. "And how will I find you?

"Leave that to me and meet me at that same shack on the coven's property. You know the one."

Oh no. The same place she'd almost died last year when she'd been kidnapped by the cold case killer. She'd barely escaped that incident. How in the hell was she going to get out of this one?

"Come alone or they both die. Your distraction should be there in minutes. Stay focused or they die. Try something heroic and they die. You've got twelve hours to get the proof and bring it to me. Do you understand?"

"Yes." She clenched her eyes shut as the call disconnected.

Sophie shoved her phone into her pants pocket and turned to find Cord showing Marshall where the other guns were stashed. Cord's phone number was the only one that the reporter had. His number was where she'd texted her new cell number. That cell number was going to be the only way she could find the reporter and the proof in time to save her friends.

Her heart raced as she steeled her nerves and walked into the living room. "Cord, do you mind if I use your phone? Mine died."

Marshall looked up from where he had his hand down behind the recliner cushion. He brought the gun out with him. He held her gaze, his assessing, and she tried not to show the fear behind her eyes.

Cord pulled his phone out and handed it to her. Marshall watched the exchange.

Sophie scanned the text messages to where Rivers had messaged the new number. She sent a text replying, "Rivers, this is Sophie. Where did you send the proof? I need to get it for my brother."

There was a pause before the answer chimed.

"There's a copy on my computer at home if Ben hasn't erased it already and another in the mail to your brother. It should be delivered in a couple of days."

"Is there security at your home?"

"Code is 1234."

Sophie rolled her eyes. "The address?"

"104 Venetian Drive."

"Computer password?"

"MenSuck."

"Thanks. I'm going over there. Ben found out about my plan, and he has my best friend. Stay safe and watch your back. If he kills me, then you're next."

Sophie closed the text and took a deep breath. Her eyes strayed to where she'd laid her purse. Her keys lay next to it. She didn't have any idea what Ben had planned, but it had better be something explosive if he didn't want Marshall to go with her. There was no way he'd let her leave without him.

She walked over to Marshall, threw her hands around his neck, and pulled him down, pressing her lips to his in a kiss she hoped looked real and lasting. He held her close to his body as he deepened the kiss, his tongue dueling with hers for purchase. She eased away. Her eyes searched his, hoping beyond anything that he could read her mind.

"Next time we visit Covington, take me to the river," she whispered against his lips.

His brows dipped.

"I'm sorry. I have to go."

Her front door burst in at that moment, and she hesitated leaving his warm embrace. Jack stormed into the living room, his gaze dead-set on Marshall. "You just had to sleep with her."

Marshall's stance widened as Jack charged him, fists swinging. The fight ensued. Furniture got broken, and all Sophie could do was ignore the fact that they were beating each other up. Cord worked to pull them apart while getting hit in the process.

Sophie eased away from the fight. She grabbed her keys and her purse before she went in a full-out run to her car. She was speeding out of the parking lot when she noticed Cord standing at her door, a confused look on his face.

Marshall pushed Cord out of the way and hurried into the parking lot.

Her phone rang seconds later as she sped out of sight. "Masterson."

"Sophie, where the hell are you going?"

"Can't talk, Marshall. Our phones are probably tapped." She hung up on him.

It rang again. "Sophie...." Marshall growled.

"Don't do this, Marshall. Lives are in danger." She hung up the phone again as she sped toward the reporter's house.

The next time it rang, she almost ignored it, only glancing at the caller ID. It read caller unknown so she answered it. "Masterson."

"Smart girl." Ben's voice sounded as cold as ice. "I do have your phones tapped."

Yeah, he might have theirs tapped, but he damn sure never had time to do anything to Cord's.

"I must say, Sophie. I didn't realize you had that much passion in you. That kiss was hot and unexpected."

"What did you tell Jack?"

"That you slept with our boss. That he fucked you the entire time we were gone. That I could hear your moans of pleasure through the thin walls while Marshall was using and abusing your body. I may have even told Jack that Marshall wanted me to video the whole event so he could watch it later. I told him you remind me of Janice the way you're whoring around."

"What did I ever do to you?" Her voice came out a whisper.

"Honey, this was never about you. This was about them. Revenge for the way they fucked me over. I lost my scholarship, and my relationship."

"With Mark?"

Ben didn't answer. "I was laughed at and ridiculed. This isn't over, Sophie. I'm going to ruin both of them. Cut them off at the knees. Take their money, their freedom, and their reputations, but first I'll start with their hearts."

"They were teens, Ben. We all go through those awkward years. Don't you think it's time to grow up?"

"Don't you dare fucking judge me, you little cunt."

"I'm coming for you, Ben. You and I will end this, or I'll die trying. Do you hear me, you little cocksucker! If you touch one hair on her head, I'll kick your balls so far up your ass, you'll never walk straight again. I'll castrate you, you son of a bitch."

"You're going to be fun to break, Sophie. If you live through this, they'll both be broken; and this time, you'll be the dead bitch tied to the bed. She was all too willing to let me tie her up. I'm going to have more fun with you, and I'll send them the video in prison. You'll be begging for me to kill you."

"Keep dreaming, you sick little fuck." Sophie hung up the phone and slid it into her pocket. Her grip tightened on the steering wheel, and her foot pressed firmly against the accelerator. She reached for the gun in her purse and snatched it out, laying it within reach. She was going to kill him.

"You have a potty mouth," Will announced, appearing right next to her.

She spared him a glance and continued driving.

"This is me, Will. Love it or leave it. I'm going to kill him."

She felt his hand on her arm and the gesture startled her. That was the first time he'd ever touched her while not in any type of dream state. His touch was warm when she'd expected it to be cold. "Sophie, I have to warn you. This is an exit point."

Sophie's foot eased off the accelerator as she pulled into the drive at River's house. She put the SUV into park. "You mean I wrote it in my chart, that I might choose to die?"

Her stomach rolled at the thought.

"It was written as an escape if your work on Earth was done."

She turned to look at him. "It's not. I'm just getting started."

"There will be pain."

"There always is," she announced as she grabbed her purse, replaced her gun inside and shoved the car door open, walking up the driveway.

He appeared beside her. His presence had returned to the ghostly apparition she was used to seeing. "There is more pain in your future. The next case may kill you."

She twisted the locked handle and bent down on her knees. She slid a credit card out of her purse and pried the door open, stepping inside seconds later to punch in the security code. "That means I'll live through this one."

She turned and grinned at Will.

"You're just dying to get back to me, aren't you?"

"Eventually," she teased, pushing away all thoughts that it was probably true. In order to return to that space and time, she would die. But that wasn't going to be today or even tomorrow. "You know you can always help me. Maybe shimmer on over and tell me if he hurt Amber or Beau."

"I can't do that." He vanished out of sight.

She ignored his reply as she went through the house, flicking on lights as she went in search of an office or the woman's computer.

She pushed open a door that led to a bedroom, and her heart practically leaped from her chest. Her eyes widened as her grip on the door tightened. A gun was pointed at her chest.

"You're just in time," Ben announced.

Sophie's gaze darted around the room. Amber's upper body was tied in a chair with her back to Beau's. Thick rope joined the two. Their mouths were duct-taped shut, their wrists bound behind their backs. One of Amber's eyes was swollen, and makeup was smeared down her face from her tears. Beau's face was bloody, and his head lulled on his shoulders. Ben stood next to Amber, one hand in her hair, yanking her head back to look at him. The other held the gun toward Sophie.

"What happened to meeting at the cabin?" she asked.

"What...and let you leave clues for the others about where to find me?"

Her mind raced. She hadn't told Marshall about the cabin. The only clue was about Rivers. He'd come looking for her, but he'd be walking into the same trap she had. Apparitions appeared in the room, making it appear smaller than the guest room actually was. First Ryan, then Macy, and last was Janice. The looks they gave her were of pity and sadness.

"Why did you drug Ryan?"

Ben's eyes narrowed. "That was meant for Jack. Jack was the one that was supposed to die."

She'd figured as much. "What good would that have done?"

"Mark could have gotten his chance to play."

She gave a slow nod, understanding more. "If you loved him, why did he leave?"

Ben gritted his teeth. "His damn father thought he was involved in the accident. He sent him away without even letting us say goodbye."

"Where is he now? Is he doing this with you?"

Ben chuckled. "No. I found out where he was and went to see him once. Can you believe he called ME a mistake! I took care of him too. But none of this would have happened if they all would have just died."

"And Janice? How does she figure into this?"

"She was a slut. Everyone knew she was doing Marshall and Jack. She didn't care." Ben's evil smirk grew wider. "It's a shame you figured this out." He shrugged. "I'm going to give them both a show they'll never forget."

He waved the gun toward the video camera staged in the room before pointing toward the bed. "Get on the bed, Sophie."

She shook her head in slow movements.

"Now!" he screamed and steadied the gun directly at her chest.

Amber tried to mouth something through her duct tape. Her words were jumbled and incoherent. She kicked out with her foot, hitting Ben in the knee. A loud crack reverted through the room, sending Ben to his knees. He tried to push himself up and aim the gun back toward Sophie. She saw his finger move to the trigger.

She had a second to move. Only one second to duck back out into the hall and take off to find another room at a dead run. The bullet missed. The hallway drywall splintered where she'd been standing. She waited for the next one.

She slid into another room and eased the door closed, her eyes adjusting to the darkness as she looked for the best place to hide. She was in the master suite. A bed, dresser, closet, and bathroom. All of the places too obvious to hide.

Sophie pulled her gun out of her purse and pressed her back into the corner behind the door. She held the gun to her chest. Her hands shook. Every noise, every creak in the house, sounded ten times louder than what was probably normal. She heard every time he used a shoulder to lean on the wall as he moved down the hall, the creaks of the other doors opening, and his cussing at finding them empty. Checking one by one, each thump against the wall louder. He was getting closer.

She closed her eyes and said a prayer, one that if she were to get killed hoped to gain her the white light she'd witnessed when dealing with the cold case serial killer. She knew what waited for her on the other side. She'd felt the love and peace that would welcome her with open arms. She wasn't afraid to die, but she preferred to live. Thoughts of Marshall flickered in her mind. Their conversations flashed in her head, as if giving her a glimpse of the life she was about to leave behind. She wasn't done. Not yet, and not with him.

She was pulled back into the present when the knob on the door turned slowly into place. The door eased open as a figure moved into the room, momentarily blocking out the light through the crack from the open door. The light returned highlighting Ben standing in the middle of the room.

"I know you're in here. Now be a good little bitch and come out so we can finish this."

Sophie held her breath, afraid to breathe. The pounding of the blood rushing into her ears was loud in her head. She was about to step out and shoot when another figure blocked out the crack of light from the hallway. This one coming from behind.

"Turn around nice and slow," Marshall threatened from the other side of the door.

Ben turned, his gun gripped in front of him. The flash of the shot and the sound of the bullet rang through the room as Ben fired.

Marshall fell to the ground with a thud. Tears clouded Sophie's vision. Her chest heaved as her heart clung to the hope that Ben was a crappy shot.

Sophie aimed and pulled the trigger, intent on emptying the clip and everything she had into killing the bastard.

More shots were fired from the doorway into Ben's body, spraying him just as she was. His body jerked with each hit until the bullets ran out. The catch of the empty clip clicked loudly in her ears. Her hands shook.

Sophie dropped her gun to the ground and fell to her knees while clutching her heart. Tears streamed down her face and her breathing was labored.

Jack walked into the room and peered around the door. He pulled her up, hugged her tightly to his chest, and ran his hand down her hair. "Don't cry, Sophie."

"He's dead. He shot Marshall." Her voice shook with her sobs.

He cupped her cheek and leaned back so he could look at her face. "No, Sophie. He's not. Marshall is fine."

She hurried around the door to find Marshall sitting up. He'd removed his shirt, and had started pulling the Velcro to unhook the Kevlar bulletproof vest. He dropped it to the floor and rubbed the forming bruise over his heart.

She dropped to her knees beside him, planted her palms on his face, and kissed him straight on the mouth. When she broke free, she leaned back. "Do that to me again and I'll kill you."

"Is that anyway to talk to your boss?"

"We both know better than that," she announced, not caring that Jack was standing behind her. She'd panicked when she glanced through the crack of the door and saw Marshall fall. She thought she'd lost him, and her world had crumbled.

Sophie helped Marshall to stand.

"So it's true? You slept with him?"

She turned to Jack. She didn't want to have this moment here, but life was too short not to. Marshall squeezed her shoulder. "I'll give you two a minute while I go help Cord untie Amber and Beau."

Sophie took a deep breath. "Nothing Ben told you was true. I haven't slept with Marshall."

She saw the instant relief on his face and yet, in two more seconds, that relief would be fleeting.

"You and I can make this work, Sophie."

She slowly shook her head. "No, we can't, Jack. We don't want the same things."

She was trying to leave the trust issues out of the equation. There was more than one reason why they shouldn't be together, and even though trust ranked up there at number one, there was more than that. "I love my job. I'm getting good at it, and I have this insane desire to help people. I only ever wanted to be loved and supported one hundred percent. I deserve that, and so do you."

He stepped closer to her and took her hands in his. "I screwed up. I know I did, but this thing between us..." He slowly shook his head. "It isn't over, Sophie. You can't love me one day and not the next. That's not how love works." He lifted her palm to rest on his chest. "You'll always be in here."

"Jack, don't do this..." she pleaded, hoping that he would have understood what she was just figuring out herself. "Don't hold hope where there isn't any."

He leaned down and pressed his lips to hers in a kiss that was meant for lovers. She softened at his touch, remembering all of the times she'd succumbed to it before. This wasn't a goodbye kiss. This kiss was a kiss that meant things were far from over. Exactly what she didn't need and adding more confusion in her heart.

A voice clearing sounded in the hallway.

Jack pulled back and ran his finger down her cheek, refusing to break their eye contact. "Remember what I said."

Jack left her standing in the doorway as he walked out, pulling a phone from his pocket. He called in the crime scene to his coworkers while Marshall pulled her into his arms. "Marshall..."

He held her tight. "Shh...you don't have to explain. I didn't expect him to back off. Hell, I wouldn't have either."

14 CHAPTER

Hours later, Sophie lay exhausted on Marshall's bed. They'd both showered, and he'd driven to her house to grab another bag since she'd insisted that Cord stay at her place instead of the neighbor's. She'd visited Amber and Beau in the hospital, both reassuring her that they would be okay. She and Amber cried while they held each other, each letting the tears flow freely.

Aiden showed up pissed off that he'd missed all of the fun and mad they'd left him out of the loop. When she explained about the phone tapping and the clues, he'd understood she had no choice. He expected to see her in the office at work so he could get back to teaching her more detailed self-defense moves. His jaw tightened, and he looked deadly as she described what Ben had been planning to do to her. The words fired up his anger as though he was ready to kill the guy again. All she'd wanted to do was shower away the memories of the day, and Marshall had brought her to his house. The video feed was still live in her home.

Marshall walked in the door and tossed her overnight bag by the bed. "Did you miss me?"

"Yes." She lay back against the pillows. "Although, if you'd been any longer, I would have fallen asleep."

He walked over to the bed and lay down next to her, his hand in her hair. He kissed her like a man starved. She took every ounce of passion that he gave her. Her body strummed to life, her nerves renewed. She wanted him.

She turned into his embrace, her hands finding purchase on his hips and trying to pull him closer. She wanted to feel him. She needed to feel him as a reminder of why she'd fought so hard to live.

He broke the kiss, leaning his forehead against hers. His jean-covered erection pressed against her belly. He took long, deep breaths as he sought composure, a feeling she was trying to find herself.

"Marshall..."

He clenched his eyes closed before opening them again to stare into hers. "Are you saying yes, Sophie?"

Her mouth parted. The words stuck in her throat.

"I didn't think so," he answered before sliding off the bed. "It's a good thing I thought ahead."

He unzipped the bag and pulled out a few of her naughty toys and tossed the bag away. "I think Bob is going to need more friends."

"You wouldn't..."

He raised and lowered his brows in quick succession. "No intercourse, but that doesn't mean I can't play. When I'm done with you, there won't be a part of your body that I haven't caressed or kissed. I plan to wear you out, Sophie Masterson."

A smile formed on her face. "That doesn't sound like much fun for you."

His grin grew. "I'll manage."

Sophie unbuttoned her jeans and slid them down her legs. "I guess we'll just see how strong that resolve is."

She kicked her jeans off and next her panties. She pulled her T-shirt over her head and lay on his bed; bare for his viewing...she ran her hands over her breasts and tweaked her own nipples before sliding her palms down over the swell of her belly and between her curls. She grinned. "I'm wet, willing, and able. Yours for the taking."

Marshall licked his lips. "You can't have me until you tell me yes." He grinned. "But I am thirsty. Let the games begin."

****

Marshall slid his fingers between Sophie's and clasped her hand as they walked into Dixon

Security. She raised their joined hands. "This isn't very professional."

His shoulders were relaxed, yet he didn't let her go. "I'm the boss."

"And I look like the gold-digging employee." She slid her fingers from his. "Talk is already going to be bad enough. Can't we wait on the PDAs?"

He chuckled. "What's wrong, Sophie? Ghosts don't scare you but a little public show of affection does?"

"I'm serious, Marshall. Your ex-girlfriend already thinks I'm using sex to get what I want. I don't need the other employees thinking the same way."

Marshall pressed the elevator call button in the garage, and they waited together, a foot apart but together. She entered the elevator and he followed. He moved to where her back was against the wall. "Alexis was just jealous." He kissed her lips and then moved his way down her neck. She watched the climbing numbers, enjoying every stolen second of his lips on her skin.

"One more floor," she announced breathlessly.

He pressed his lips to hers once more. "You know, I'm going to have to rectify this. I'm not sure I can keep my hands off of you in the office. How about we move you to the office next to mine and we get an adjoining door?"

She chuckled, pressing her palm to his chest and moving him back.

"How about not."

Sophie led the way out of the elevator, Marshall walking next to her. She lifted a hand to her belly, unable to stop her butterflies. "The others are going to hate me. I killed their friend."

"No they're not, Sophie. He betrayed us. All of us." He placed his palm on her back and guided her farther up the hall. "A couple of the IT girls may, but not the guys."

She stopped, and Marshall grinned. "That's a joke. It was just a joke, Sophie."

"That wasn't funny."

He chuckled. "Sure it was. Let's go or we're going to be late."

The walked into the conference room where Aiden and the others were waiting. Beau's face looked better. Well, cleaned up anyway. He had bandages over the bad areas, a busted lip, and a black eye. But he was alive, and that was all that mattered.

Beau held her gaze and nodded before they all sat down, everyone in their spot, as it had been the first day.

Silently, Roman stood up at the end of the table and they all turned toward him. "Sophie. No one blames you for what happened. You did what you had to. Marshall and Beau are my family, and you saved them both. That makes you a member too."

"Does she even know what that means?" Dash asked.

KATE ALLENTON

"Um...thanks, Roman." She glanced at Marshall, who was leaning back in his chair. His lips broadened into a smile that hinted at humor. "Does this mean family dinners? Because I suck at cooking. Just ask my brother."

Aiden cleared his throat and turned accusingly to Marshall. "You didn't tell her?"

"Nope, I was leaving it up to all of you to decide. I can see the decision has been made."

They all nodded in agreement.

"Okay...what's the secret? What aren't you telling me?"

"Every member sitting at this table is a co-owner in my company. We started it together. My shares top theirs, but we each have an equal vote," he said to her before glancing at all of the others. They nodded. "It appears you just made partner."

Sophie didn't think she could be any more surprised than she'd already been that they weren't blaming her for Ben's death. But she'd never guessed they were all co-owners. Never guessed that this group of men would accept her, flaws and all.

A tear escaped her clouded eyes. "You guys believe in me?" Her voice came out a whisper.

"It's more than that," Dash explained. "We'll always have your back. You can count on us."

"No matter what," Roman said.

"No matter when," Aiden added.

"No matter where or why," Beau finished.

Sophie swiped at the tear. For the first time in her life, she felt accepted. She felt supported. She felt like an equal, and when she glanced at Marshall, she felt loved.

"Hoorah?" she answered and laughter filled the room.

Champagne was brought in and poured into crystal glasses.

Will, Ryan, Macy and Janice appeared in the corner of the room. Each at ease, with smiling faces, though they remained quiet.

"You did well." Will announced and the others nodded.

Sophie held up her champagne flute in a toast. "My each of you now rest in peace."

Nothing was accomplished that day. No one worked. Everyone took one day, enjoying each other and life without threats, exes, or killers. Life was too precious to let slip by. Life was meant to be lived, and she damn sure was going to live hers.

Sneak Peek at the next book Veiled
Intentions currently available on Amazon.

Chapter 1

Sophie pasted the sweetest smile she could
muster on her face as she passed the receptionist at
the police department. There was nothing unusual
about her visits. Her brother was chief after all.

"Where are they?" she asked.

Veronica grinned and tilted her head toward the
conference room door. "Boy, what I wouldn't give
to be a fly on the wall."

Sophie pressed her lips together and headed
toward where the traitors were meeting. She swung
the door open and placed her hand on her hip.
"What did I miss?"

The exchanged glances would have been
comical if the reason they were meeting wasn't as
important as it was. The Pentagram Killer was back
and had struck again.

Marshall rose. "Sophie, what are you doing
here? I thought you were having lunch with
Amber."

"Our lunch meeting got pushed back." She let
her gaze scan the room, noting her brother, Jack,

and Cord were in there too. "It's a good thing too. I might have missed this."

Jack rose from his seat. "Uh uh, no way in hell is she helping on this one."

"Sit down, Love," Max ordered before her brother returned his gaze back to Marshall, her boyfriend slash boss. She'd expected Jack's protest, and maybe a little from her brother if she was being honest, but the fact that they'd tried to blackball her out of this case had her every nerve ending on fire. If she had superpowers, she'd be shooting cobwebs out of her hands to cover their mouths to keep them from lying to her face. "She's not doing this."

An apparition appeared in the room standing at the other end of the table. The boisterous woman that Sophie had met previous times while learning about her clairvoyance was standing in the standard-issue white coven dress. A dress that Sophie knew all too well. The apparition wasn't just a member of the coven. She had been the *leader* of the coven.

"He struck again?" she asked, turning her gaze to Marshall. He didn't reply. So she turned her questioning to her brother. "Mary James," she stated more than asked. "Head of the local coven."

Jack's eyes narrowed. "How do you know that? It isn't public information."

Marshall leaned back in his chair, a half-grin on his face, trying to hide the pride from showing in his eyes. "Do you even have to ask, Jack?"

Sophie blew Marshall a kiss before gesturing toward the end of the table. "She's standing right there." Sophie put her hand on the doorknob and grinned. "I guess since I wasn't invited to your little party, I'll go have my own."

She wiggled her fingers as she turned. "Later, boys."

Sophie spun on her heels and stormed out of the building. She slid into the back seat of the waiting Dixon Security SUV. Beau was behind the wheel, Amber next to him. Aiden grinned sitting next to her. "How did it go?"

"You know…" was her only reply with a shoulder shrug.

Amber turned around in her seat. "That good?"

"You have to give Cord a break because he's new, but the others… They should have known better than to try leaving you out," Beau announced.

Aiden laid his arm across the back of the seat. "Oh, I don't know. I can see why they're worried about her. Their only mistake is underestimating my mad teaching skills."

"Conceited much?" Beau asked as he held Aiden's gaze through the rearview mirror.

"She can take your ass." Aiden smirked.

"Any time, any place," Beau replied.

Amber tapped Beau on the arm. "You are not allowed to hurt my best friend."

"But, baby…he's practically daring me."

"I'm not afraid of him, Amber." She turned to wink at Aiden. "Aiden is that good."

"That's my girl." He rubbed her shoulder. "So where are we going for lunch?"

"Mexican," they all replied at the same time.
****

Twenty minutes later they were seated at their favorite local restaurant with a plate of the best nachos in town sitting in front of each of them. The heavenly, melted cheesy, gooeyness was too good to share.

"You know what I don't get," Sophie said. "How they thought they could keep me out of it."

Beau shrugged. "The Pentagram Killer is dangerous and elusive. I'm sure they were just worried."

Sophie took a sip of her sweet iced tea. "You guys aren't."

"Think about who was in the meeting, Soph. Your ex-boyfriend, your new boyfriend, your brother, and your new trainee, who by the way deserves a good reprimand for not warning you. You are a partner after all. Marshall should have brought it to the table. We should have agreed as a unit."

"Marshall does own majority share, regardless of the rest of our equal votes," she countered.

"He's also thinking with his johnson instead of his head," Aiden said as he glanced at her. "If you were my girlfriend, I wouldn't want you anywhere near the case either."

"Good thing I'm not." She smirked and leaned back in the booth, her food momentarily forgotten. "This was exactly what I was afraid would happen."

Amber swallowed the nacho in her mouth. "You can always break up with him. It's not like he's giving you any."

Aiden and Beau paused with chips halfway to their mouths as they turned to stare at her with wide eyes.

"You had to go there," Sophie relied as she looked at her best friend.

"What? It's the truth. He brings a whole new meaning to phrase 'You better put a ring on it'."

"Is that why you've been so cranky?" Beau's lips twitched. "You need to get laid?"

Aiden slid his arm around her shoulders and squeezed her into his side. "Do you need me to take the edge off? It can be our little secret."

"I suggest your remove your hand if you intend to keep it, Aiden," Marshall announced as he strolled up to the table. He pulled a chair over to their booth and twisted it around to sit backwards on it. Marshall was a good-looking man. He looked great every day, but there was something special about him today. Was it that she was seeing him through rose colored glasses?

Aiden removed his hand but kept his shit-eating grin as he did. "Just thought you might need some help with your girl." Aiden glanced at Beau before returning his gaze to Marshall. "We hear you aren't performing."

"Oh, for the love of god." Sophie's face reddened as she cupped it in her hand. "I did not say that."

Marshall took one of Sophie's nachos and shoved the entire thing in his mouth. He chewed and swallowed before standing. Leaning over her, he pressed his hot mouth to hers in a kiss that could make her forget they were in public. He tasted of cheese and gooeyness and everything she loved. His kiss made her body ache. A moan slipped from her lips. His fingers glided over her neck before tangling in her hair. There was no hesitation, only a deepening and demanding as his tongue glided into her mouth, possessing and making her question her hesitation on giving into the one thing he wanted. A simple yes, and he'd take her. A simple yes, and he'd fill her. A simple yes, and her life wouldn't be her own.

She pressed at his chest, and she felt his grin against her lips. He didn't budge, but he ended the kiss with a few nibbles on her lower lip. Her cheeks flushed and her lips tingled. "I'm mad at you."

"I know," he whispered while leaning his forehead against hers. "I'm sorry."

Sophie chewed her lip for a split second before she grinned. "Apology accepted. Don't be an idiot again."

Marshall pressed a tiny kiss to her lips before righting his stance. He lifted his hand to his heart. "Scout's honor."

"I seriously doubt you were a scout," she teased.

The twinkle in his eyes hinted that she was right. "I'll fill you in on the file when you get back to the office. Keep your paws off my girl," Marshall called over his shoulder as he turned and headed out of the restaurant.

"I'll think about it," Aiden hollered back, turning in the booth.

"Dude…" Sophie picked up another nacho and pulled at the cheese on top. "Don't poke the bear.

He's just as sexually frustrated as I am, if not more." She grinned.

****

Sophie arrived back at work and dropped her purse off behind her desk before heading to Marshall's office. She held Cord's gaze as she walked by his desk. Ignoring his six-foot-two frame and the familiar lethal look he always outwardly projected. She gestured, pointing from her eyes back to his in quick succession. "You and me…later."

Marshall's door was open. He stood behind his desk, looking out of the tinted floor-to-ceiling window to the street down below. She took a minute to admire him as he looked lost in thought, his large hands clasped behind his back. His dark Armani suit was tailored to fit every inch of his body. The material was expensive and beautiful but didn't compare to the man wearing it.

"Like the view?" he asked.

"It's better than yours," she answered as she walked up behind him. She gazed down in the same direction he'd been looking to figure out what was holding his attention.

"He could be anyone," Marshall announced out of the blue. "We don't even have a name, much less a face to look for."

"He could be a she," Sophie countered.

"Doubt it." Marshall moved to stand behind her and wrapped his arms around her waist. He rested his head on her shoulder before placing a tiny kiss on her neck. "She'd have to be a bodybuilder due to the sheer size of the guys killed over the years, not to mention the positions they were left in."

Sophie placed her arms on top of Marshall's and stroked circles, enjoying the feel of the material. Her gaze was drawn to the white dove that landed on the windowsill. "We may be looking at a team."

Marshall raised his head to look at the side of her face. "Why do you say that?"

She shrugged and turned to steal a kiss. "Only another harmless-looking female could have gotten close enough to lure Mary away from her coven."

She turned in his arms and laced her fingers behind his neck. "You need me."

"I've known that since the first day I met you."

She lifted on her tiptoes and pressed another kiss to his lips. "That's not what I meant. You need me on this case."

She cupped his cheeks and stole another kiss before she sidestepped him and headed for the door. "Family meeting in thirty minutes, we vote." She turned at the last minute and grinned. "I already have three votes in my pocket, so get ready to concede."

"Sophie. Do what you will, but you're the one that may be eating crow." Marshall's eyes glinted with secrets, his smile assuring her that he meant what he said.

"Marshall, honey, there isn't much that can surprise me."

"We'll see." He winked before turning back toward the window and reassuming the position he'd been in before she interrupted.

ABOUT THE AUTHOR

Kate has lived in Florida for most of her entire life. She enjoys a quiet life with her husband, Michael and two kids.

Kate has pulled all-nighters finishing her favorite books and also writing them. She says she'll sleep when she's dead or when her muse stops singing off key.

She loves creating worlds full of suspense, secrets, hunky men, kick ass heroines, steamy sex and oh yeah the love of a lifetime. Not to mention an occasional ghost and other supernatural talents thrown into the mix.